In one swift movement, Prince John swung himself out of the saddle and jumped to the ground in front of me. "Something has driven me irresistibly to this very spot," he said.

"I cannot imagine what that could be, Your Grace."

"Can you not, fair maiden?" His eyebrows shot up and his grin widened boyishly.

"My lord!" I turned away from him. "I have not the least idea. The flowers perhaps." I stooped, picked up a spray of asters, and held them to my breast.

"A flower," he said, looking deep into my eyes. "A flower far lovelier than any that grows in the field. Thou art the flower, fairest maiden. The fairest flower of all."

Astonished at his courtly phrases, I could not speak nor could I meet the intensity of his eyes. I stood, at a loss for words, gazing at the flowers that I held in my hand.

"What is your name, sweet maiden?" Prince John asked.

"Elaine."

SILVER JEWELS AND JADE

ELIZABETH NORMAN

BALLANTINE BOOKS • NEW YORK

Library of Congress Catalog Card Number: 79-57463

ISBN 0-345-28671-5

Manufactured in the United States of America

First Edition: May 1980

Author's Note

❋❋❋❋❋❋❋❋❋❋❋❋❋❋❋❋❋❋❋❋❋

"There are two sides to every story" states the cliché. This is particularly true of *Silver, Jewels and Jade* in that it is composed of two autobiographical accounts of the same events, written by two stepsisters, Gloria and Elaine. Though each narrative is complete in itself, each adds to the significance of the other.

Elaine's account has been known for years, but no one, to my knowledge, had ever suspected the existence of Gloria's. I discovered it quite by accident while staying with my friends Julia and Adrian Hillery at Swans' Lodge, their fifteenth-century manor house near Devygorth, Wales. I could not believe at first that I had found a counterpart to Elaine's story in that remote place, and I shall always be indebted to Julia and Adrian for allowing me to rummage through their chests of old manuscripts, where I discovered it.

I was familiar with Elaine's story. Lord Toddingdale of Cranshaw Hall in Devon had translated it from the Middle English in 1856, and it has remained a curiosity in the library there ever since. The account is obscure in many respects, and it was not until my dramatic discovery of Gloria's manuscript that certain aspects of Elaine's life were clarified.

In its original Middle English, Gloria's account begins:

Whan I was to the Castel Idris commen, myn moder cleped me Igraine. But I was highte Gloria. Aboven al thinges, I wolde witen what maade her clepen me thus. And I wolde kennen for why she broghte me ther.

Most readers would never stand for this, so I have translated her manuscript into contemporary language that is compatible, I believe, with Lord Toddingdale's translation of Elaine's story.

Elaine is more familiar to us as Igraine, who in later life was to have such an effect upon Uther Pendragon. But this is the story of her maidenhood, so we need not concern ourselves with that here.

Unfortunately Elaine's original manuscript is lost. Whether Lord Toddingdale destroyed it after having translated it (I cannot believe he would have done such a thing), or whether it was inadvertently discarded or simply lost, we do not know. Perhaps it will reappear one day. But not having it to compare with Lord Toddingdale's translation, we can only guess what liberties he took with the original.

Liberties he did take. Details that are inconsistent with the period—whether Elaine was originally called Igraine, Igerne, or Ygaerne, or whether it was John or Gorlois who was to become King of Tintagal or Duke of Tintagal—will be apparent to scholars. These questions are of little interest to us, but the death of Mathilda is another matter in that it is obviously a complete invention. I suppose it was written by Lord Toddingdale in one of his romantic Victorian moods. The account is so delightful, however, that I have left it as he wrote it.

The description of Mathilda's death, which appeared in Elaine's original manuscript, is entirely different. It exists among Lord Toddingdale's papers, and I include it here in an afterword.

Finally, instead of presenting the two narratives consecutively, I have taken the liberty of inserting Gloria's story into Elaine's in three sections, thereby preserving the dramatic chronology of the whole.

Newport, January 1979

Chapter One

✦✦✦✦✦✦✦✦✦✦✦✦✦✦✦✦✦✦✦

Elaine's Story

"It did not go that way," the man said.

Fang began to growl. I silenced the dog by glaring and raising my staff at him.

"Not a blade of grass is crushed," he continued. "Not a hoof print in the ground there. Not a broken branch. The beast did not go that way. Yet you said it did."

"I did not speak a word, my lord," I said, looking up at the man on his white horse.

"You nodded in that direction."

The man pointed with his spear to the edge of the meadow where a ragged hedge of oak saplings screened the forest. But he did not look in that direction. Instead, his arm extended imperiously, he stared down at me with narrowed, startlingly brilliant blue eyes.

I did not hurry to reply, but took a moment to examine him. He was a big man, though young—perhaps eighteen or twenty years old. His features were handsome: high cheekbones, straight nose, and heavy chin. Unruly black hair curled low over his forehead. He wore a scarlet surcoat lined with ermine, and spurs of gold.

"Surely, sir knight," I said, "I may look where I please. If you chose to construe a glance as a direction, it was no fault of mine. Now I shall not move at all lest you misinterpret me further."

"You are insolent, maiden!" he said. "Take care!"

He lowered the spear and grasped the reins with both hands to quiet his horse. But he seemed unable to look away from my face. As I returned his stare, I thought how silent the air had become—the meadow and the wood seemed to hold their breath. Then a curlew cried from somewhere far away and broke the spell.

"You act rightly, maiden," the knight continued at last. "Do not move, then, if that motion be a lie and show your ignorance in the bargain. I have never seen so large a boar nor one so fierce. The animal would be dead this moment had you shown me where it ran. Why do you protect such an evil creature? So that it may attack the weary pilgrim on the road or the shepherd on the hillside? Have you more love of boars and pigs than of men? How well your labor suits you, then."

"The boar has done you no harm, my lord. And I have no love of swine. It is no desire of mine to tend them. An evil man forces to do so. But I would rather bear the obstinacy of a pig ten thousand times than the cruelty of a man for a moment."

The rider did not answer me. But, with a sneer, almost before I had finished speaking, he spurred his horse forward and galloped away across the meadow, followed by his squire and two archers who had kept apart from us as we had spoken.

It was with strange, mixed feelings—of anger and almost of shame or embarrassment—that I watched the knight and his companions ride down the steep hillside meadow to the road, some thirty feet below me. They turned to the left when they reached it and vanished almost at once as the road curved out of sight into a wooded valley behind the hill.

Why did I feel so disturbed? A few minutes earlier an enormous wild boar, about to drop from exhaustion, had run up the hill and past me. It looked at me pitifully! Then the hunting party galloped up out of nowhere, and when the knight asked me which way the beast had gone, I could not bear to tell him. Had I acted foolishly? No, I was glad the boar was alive.

I had no doubt that if the knight had overtaken the animal it would be dead now. The stranger's powerful shoulders, the massive arms that bulged beneath the tight sleeves of his tunic, his thick wrists and huge hands all foretold the power behind his spear's thrust.

I had seen this boar many times, standing motionless in the shadow of thicket or wood, staring at me. But it had never approached—never annoyed me or the pigs. Fang would growl at the beast, but he never ran after it; he left it entirely alone.

Though I was glad that the boar still lived, I feared the knight had thought me an idiot. Perhaps that was what bothered me. But did it matter what he thought? Who was he, and why had he been hunting so near Castle Idris?

As if to answer my question, trumpets sounded in the distance—from the direction the hunting party had taken, I thought. Then I heard a low, muffled drone rather like that of many flying insects. It was ominous. It grew louder. Again I heard the trumpets blare, and then I knew what the strange noise was. It was the rumble of horses' hoofs on the ground, not just a few horses but a great many of them—perhaps a hundred.

What was happening? Were we being attacked? Would some neighboring duke besiege the castle? Frightened, I watched the road.

Then, led by the trumpeters, a procession marched slowly into view from behind the hill and proceeded down the road toward the castle. Fifty spearmen and archers in scarlet livery rode behind the trumpeters. Then mounted noblemen, knights, gentlemen and their squires and henchmen appeared; grooms and priests; household officials, some mounted and some on foot; huntsmen, falconers, clerks, yeomen, and pack horses. Fifty more spearmen and archers rode behind, concluding the train.

The party must have numbered a hundred and fifty or more. But it was not a war party. No, a wealthy lord was on his way to visit Castle Idris. I could tell this by the apparel of the nobles and knights and by their demeanor. They wore no armor, but sat astride their beautifully caparisoned mounts, dressed in tunics and cloaks of brilliant hues and trimmed with fur, bejeweled, and embroidered in gold. They laughed and talked freely together.

In their midst, yet set apart, rode their lord on his white horse. He was the young man who had hunted the boar and to whom I had spoken. He wore his scarlet surcoat still, but now he also wore a tall, square fur hat. A gold and jeweled sword flashed and sparkled at his side.

He looked up at me as he passed—a long, lingering gaze beneath a dark frown, I thought, though he was too far away for me to be sure. Then he turned away, never looking back again.

I watched him and his party travel down the parched road that cleaved the long meadows, now purple with wild autumn asters, sloping ever toward the sea. Behind them in the yellow afternoon light, the dust of their passage rose in a plume of gold.

I watched until he became a tiny speck and the procession had crossed the marshes, laced with silver where the sunlight lay reflected in the brackish water. Then the company climbed the hill to the drawbridge and passed through the gateway of Castle Idris, the castle which long ago had been my home.

How long ago? Forever ago. So long that my life there hardly seemed real to me any more. But my suffering on leaving the castle was still terribly real. I could never forget that, nor the grim years that had followed that awful day ten years before. Nor could I forget Sir Tor Malafie, the horrible man who was responsible for it all. Sir Tor would never allow me to forget.

Now I lived outside the castle at the farm, a mean cluster of buildings that cowered against the base of the castle's outer wall. I was the swineherd and I lived in the swineherd's hut, a low hovel of mud and sticks with a thatched roof. I could see it from where I sat.

Above it soared the wall of the castle's outer bailey. Like the rest of Castle Idris, it was built of white limestone. It ringed the castle's hillock like a silver collar. High on the hilltop a second towered wall encircled the inner bailey. This was a wide, open space which surrounded many buildings huddled together. Their roofs rose ever higher, forming a great cone which almost enveloped the four towers of the keep. On stormy days when the sky hung low, these immense towers pierced the clouds.

But no storm threatened the azure sky that day. Castle Idris sat serenely on its emerald hill. Its white turrets and towers, gilded by the autumn sun, gleamed against an endless sapphire sea.

I sat in the meadow until the dust of the procession had settled on the road, gazing at the glorious scene before me and trying not to think of anything but its beauty. Then Fang and I collected my herd of pigs and drove them before us down the hillside path to the road and then to the farm and into their pen.

As I walked, I prayed that I would not see Sir Tor that evening. I tried to think of other things, but dreaded to find him waiting for me or coming upon me. My dread gave me no peace. But surely he would be too occupied that night to bother me. The lordly knight's party was a large one, and as steward of Castle Idris, Sir Tor would be busy seeing to its accommodation and comfort.

But I was not so fortunate.

Chapter Two

✠✠✠✠✠✠✠✠✠✠✠✠✠✠✠✠✠✠

Elaine's Story

As I sat alone in my hut at dusk, a sheepskin wrapped about me, I heard footsteps on the ground outside. The door was thrown open, and there in the doorway stood Sir Tor Malafie.

He stood in silhouette against the dim evening light of the farmyard. He was a short man and vain, like so many short men. In his youth he had developed his stubby body to massive proportions with exercise. But now he was past his fortieth year, and his huge arms and muscular torso had become thick and corpulent. His vast belly, however, had not diminished his brutal strength.

"No fire, Elaine?" he demanded, stepping into the room.

Fang, who lay beside the doorway, began to growl. Sir Tor looked down at him for a moment, and then kicked the dog in the side. Fang staggered to his feet and ran yelping from the hut.

"Build a fire," Sir Tor said to me. "Light this miserable— Give you light. Keep you warm."

"I have been in the hills tending the swine all day, Sir Tor," I said, standing up and facing him, "as you must know. I have had little time to build fires, and since I am tired and about to retire, I see no point in building one now. And besides, little smoke passes through that." I pointed to the hole in the roof. "I would rather breathe cold, clean air than choke to death."

"Humph," Sir Tor snorted. "You'll catch your death." He closed the door and walked unsteadily toward me. "Build a fire!" He smelled of wine and perspiration.

"Thank you for your concern, Sir Tor. But I hardly expected to see you tonight. There must be a great deal to do at the castle."

"Prince John of Tintagal. You know about that?"

"With a hundred and fifty visitors? How could one help knowing? I heard about it at supper."

"Prince John of Tintagal," Sir Tor repeated. "Come to see the Lady Gloria. All fed and quartered. And His Grace and the lady all alone by now, no doubt. And who is to say what they might be doing together, eh?"

Sir Tor laughed and nodded his head knowingly. His heavy jowls shook. I could see their outline in the dim light, but I could not see his eyes—those shrewd, watery, little gray eyes, so like a pig's.

"Just back from Palestine is Prince John," Sir Tor continued. "I told him how I won the war horse at the tournament at Ashland. None could unhorse me that day. My lance was invincible. I was the bravest, most valiant knight on the lists."

He went on bragging about his bravery and telling about the knights he had left bleeding on the field. It was a tale he had told me fifty times before. And then he described how he had lifted the biggest ox in the yard on his shoulders without help when no other man could do it. This I had also heard many times before.

Finally he stopped talking. He slapped his thigh,

glared about the hut, and said, "Give us a little wine, Elaine. My throat is dry from our conversation."

"I have no wine, Sir Tor. How would I have wine?"

"No wine and hardly a rag on your back when you know how easy it would be to live like a queen. You have only to marry me. I will dress you as fine as I. Feel my coat—the finest cashmere and trimmed with pearls."

He grasped my hand and placed it upon his chest. I felt something sticky there—gravy, I thought.

"I will dress you in gowns of silk and velvet and in furs. I will give you a proper chamber to sleep in. And I will be kind to you. See? I have brought you a present to keep you warm."

He held up a bundle which he had carried tucked under his arm. Now he shook it out. It was a cloak, and he held it open as if to put it about me.

"Turn around," he commanded.

I did so, and he removed the sheepskin I still wore. Then I felt the warm weight of the cloak fall about my shoulders. I pulled it close about me, stroking its soft wool.

Then I felt his arms curl about me. Turning me to face him, he grasped me to him and kissed me on the mouth. I thought the long kiss would never end. I held my breath and tried not to think of his rotting teeth. He finished finally, and crushed me to him, the stubble of his chin pricking my neck.

"Please, you are hurting me," I said.

"Marry me, Elaine," he murmured, hugging me even tighter. "You will in the end. You must!" He released me from his embrace, but clutched my arms still. "I have been good to you. I have been kind to you—understanding. Please, Elaine," he whined. "Please! I have tried to make you understand me. I have been patient. I have waited all these years. But you are a young woman now. Please, Elaine. What have I done to make you dislike me so? You do not understand me, Elaine. Marry me! Let us live together. Come to understand me. Come to love me."

His fingers tightened on my arms until I thought I must cry out in pain, and I could see in my mind that cold glint of cruelty in his eyes which frightened me so.

"No. No, I cannot. I—"

" 'You cannot. You cannot,' " he mimicked. "Always the same: 'You cannot.' But you *will*."

I did cry out then. "Stop it! Stop it! You are hurting me."

"You *will* marry me, won't you," he growled.

What could I say? What excuse could I make this time? How could I extricate myself without angering him further?

I had no need to say anything; Brian, the smith, rescued me. I had not heard the door open, nor had Sir Tor.

"Elaine?" Brian said.

Sir Tor released me and I shrank from him.

"Smith?" Sir Tor roared at Brian. "What do you want? What brings you here at *night?*"

"I . . . I . . . "

"You? You *what!*" Sir Tor bellowed.

"I came to find Elaine. I— The night is cold, and . . . on cold nights she sleeps by my forge."

He fell silent. The two men stood facing each other for several moments without speaking.

"This is no place for her," Brian continued. "Not on winter nights. One cold room . . . Not in the summer is it fit. She is a child still. Surely—"

"If she does not build a fire, it is no fault of mine," Sir Tor cried.

"No, sir knight. Surely not, sir knight. But—"

"You tell me that I am cruel?" Sir Tor almost whispered the words. "You tell me that I treat her badly?"

"No! Good and noble knight! No, you have been kindness itself."

"See the cloak I have given her to keep her warm," Sir Tor said.

Again the two men stood facing each other in silence.

Then Sir Tor said in a low growl, "So you creep here in the night and take my betrothed to your house and bed her down by your fireside, eh?"

"Sir Tor!" Brian cried. "You yourself have bidden me look after her."

"I am not your betrothed, Sir Tor," I said.

Sir Tor whirled and faced me. "You are!" he shouted. "You were given to me ten years ago. You know that! Everyone knows that. Isn't that so, smith?"

"Yes, Sir Tor," Brian said. "It is true, sir knight."

"And she will marry me! Never forget it, smith: that this is my *wife*."

"I shall never give my consent, Sir Tor," I said as calmly as I could. "I shall never be your wife. I have told you that many times. So long as my consent is required, I shall never marry you. And I shall never change my mind. Why do you persecute me, then? Have not you punished me enough? I have been given my choice: that was agreed. I have chosen. I shall remain here with the swine."

"And sleep with this rutting dog?" Sir Tor shouted.

"That is unfair, Sir Tor," I cried. "Brian and his wife have been kind to me and helped me. You *ordered* them to. Now will you berate them for obeying you?"

Sir Tor turned back to Brian. "Take care, smith," he whispered, his voice quavering. "Do not betray me." He paused. "For if you do, you may follow all the rest."

He paused again before one final deadly threat.

Chapter Three

Elaine's Story

Slowly and deliberately, Sir Tor said, "And who will there be to save you?"

He stood facing Brian for a moment. Then, as if fate propelled the two men like puppets, Brian stepped out of Sir Tor's path, and Sir Tor strode through the doorway and out into the night.

I went to Brian. I felt him trembling when I laid my hand on his arm. "Do not be afraid, dear Brian," I said.

Tears flooded my eyes. Sir Tor had never made me cry—except for that first day. But I had been a child then. I cried now for Brian, though, because I knew what a kind, sensitive man he was. He had been like a father to me—as much a one as he could be, that is, without incurring Sir Tor's wrath. It made me cry to feel this sweet, huge, brawny man tremble with fear.

"Don't be afraid," I repeated. "I will not let anything happen to you."

"Could you stop him?" Brian asked. "Would you marry him to stop him?"

I was speechless with the horror of Brian's question.

"I would not let you do that, my dear," he continued, "even if my life depended on it. But . . . " He shivered violently. "But I dare not think what he could do to me if he wished. There is no one left to protect us. If your father should return, how many men would he know here now? And what would happen to my dear Gueneth if I were gone?"

"Don't, Brian," I said. "It is not going to happen. He would not dare send you away. He would not hurt you. You are the best smith living. He *needs* you. He was angry because of me. It was merely talk. But I *would* marry him to save you. I would not let anything happen to you, dear friend."

"Should you not marry him anyway?" Brian asked.

"Brian!" I cried. "How can you think such a thing?"

"But surely you could come to manage him somehow. You cannot go on living like this—like the animals you tend. In the coldest weather they sleep with you, in this very room!"

"Rather that than with Sir Tor, Brian—unless I must. Now let us talk of other things. Yes, I will gladly sleep by the forge tonight. Dear Brian, thank you. Will you carry my pallet? And I will take the skins."

As we walked across the yard toward the smithy, I said, "Is it truly Prince John of Tintagal visiting here?"

"Yes," Brian said. "Have you seen him?"

"From— from the hillside. I saw them all pass by. So many men! It will mean long hours of work for you, won't it? Poor Brian."

"I do not mind. I like work, and the time passes quickly. I like to shape the iron and know that it will stay that way once it cools—the way I made it. But I have told you that before."

He smiled down at me, his teeth gleaming in the moonlight. The moon had risen in the late afternoon, and now it shone down on us from the dark sky, lighting our way.

"Yes, and I never tire of hearing it. I like the happiness in your voice when you tell it."

We walked on in silence until we reached the smithy. Brian opened the doors for me, and I stepped into the warm room. The fire, banked for the night, glowed and flickered, casting a dull glow on the anvil, on Brian's hammers and tongs, and on some pieces of old ironwork that hung on pegs on the wall.

He arranged my pallet before the fire and then said, "Good night, Elaine. Sleep well. Do not think about Sir Tor tonight. You will be safe from him here."

"I doubt that, Brian. I doubt that we are safe from him anywhere." But then, sorry that I had uttered such a gloomy thought, and hoping to make Brian forget it, I asked, "Did he come to see Gloria?"

"Prince John?" Brian responded. "Why should he do that?"

"Sir Tor said he did."

"Come to see the Lady Gloria?" Brian snorted. "He'd as soon go to see the hag of Prydwen, I should think. He came to hunt. At least that is what they say. Good night. Gueneth will wonder where I am."

With that he left me. I removed my cloak, folded it carefully, and set it on a stool. Then I lay down on my pallet and drew a sheepskin over me. But it was a long time before sleep came; thoughts of Sir Tor kept it at bay.

The following morning I herded my pigs back to the hillside where I had seen Prince John the day before. A little farther along the slope, at the edge of the forest, beeches and oaks supplied plentiful acorns and beechmast.

There I sat in the shelter of a big rock, out of the north wind, where I could look down at the castle and the ocean. The day was a copy of the one before, clear and sunny. It was so warm in the sun away from the wind that I removed the cloak that Sir Tor had given me and laid it aside.

As I did so, I wondered if I should have kept it. But I had kept all the gifts he had given me. I could not have lived without them. The very mattress that I slept on, the sheepskins that covered me were gifts from him. Since he had destroyed my world, I had never had any compunction about accepting things he gave me. Why, then, should I make an exception now?

I was so engrossed in my thoughts and the grassy ground was so soft that I did not hear the rider approach until he was almost upon me.

Chapter Four

✠✠✠✠✠✠✠✠✠✠✠✠✠✠✠✠✠✠

Elaine's Story

Prince John sat still in the saddle, looking down at me without speaking.

I rose and said, "Good morning, Your Grace."

"Ah," he said, "you know who I am."

"Yes, my lord. I should think everyone at the castle does."

He frowned at me. But somehow I did not think he was angry—it was a mock frown, I felt.

"Have you seen a wild boar with huge tusks come crashing through the brush near here?"

"No, my lord. I have not seen it today, and I am sorry about yesterday."

"Oh? You are sorry? Why are you sorry?"

"Because . . . " I picked up my new cloak and threw it about my shoulders. I could not help thinking that its green color became me. "Because there is something about that animal. I think it came to me for protection. At least it must have known that you could not follow its tracks where my swine had trod the ground. I . . . "

"Yes?" the prince asked.

"I think it is a very old boar, and I could not refuse to help it."

"It is but an animal."

"Perhaps."

Now the prince smiled. "Perhaps? Do you think it more? Do you think it bewitched?"

"I do not know, my lord. But I do not think it is an ordinary animal. There is something about its eyes— something about the way it looks at me sometimes. But I am sorry I could not direct you to it."

Now Prince John grinned broadly. It was a charming smile, and I was enchanted by the brilliant, sparkling blueness of his eyes and the way the skin about them crinkled.

Then suddenly, in one swift movement, he swung himself out of the saddle and jumped to the ground in front of me. I was amazed that a man of his size could be so nimble.

Flinging the reins to his squire, who rode forward instantly to grasp them, he said, "In so doing, you have given me something more intriguing. Something far lovelier than this beautiful place." He swung his arm to encompass the view. "Something that has driven me irresistibly to this very spot."

"I cannot imagine what that could be, Your Grace."

"Can you not, fair maiden?" His eyebrows shot up and his grin widened boyishly.

"My lord!" I turned away from him. "I have not the least idea. The flowers perhaps." I stooped, picked a spray of asters, and held them to my breast.

"*A* flower," he said, looking deep into my eyes. "A flower far lovelier than any that grows in the field. Thou art the flower, fairest maiden. The fairest flower of all."

Astonished at his courtly phrases, I could not speak nor could I meet the intensity of his eyes. I stood, at a loss for words, gazing at the flowers that I held in my hand.

"What is your name, sweet maiden?" Prince John asked.

"Elaine."

"Then there are two Elaines in this enchanted place."

"Two Elaines?" I asked, looking up at him now.

"The Lady Elaine, daughter of the Duke of Idris, and Elaine the swineherd."

"They are one and the same, Your Grace."

Now he frowned, not with anger, but with intense interest. "One and the same?"

"Yes, my lord. My father was the Duke of Idris and I am the swineherd."

"That is not possible."

"Why is it not possible, my lord?"

"Because I dined with the Lady Elaine last night at the castle and with her stepmother, Dame Idris."

"Dame Idris is *my* stepmother, my lord. If you dined with a Lady Elaine, it was not her stepdaughter because she has no other stepdaughter by that name."

"Pray be seated, maiden," the prince said.

I sat down on a rock.

Then Prince John threw himself down beside me, and after he had gazed at me for a moment or two, he said gently, "Now tell me why you believe that you are Elaine, daughter of the Duke of Idris."

"Because he was my father," I said, looking straight into Prince John's eyes. "I grew up living here in the castle with my father and mother, whose name was also Elaine. I am her namesake. She died at Castle Clydach, our castle in Wales, when I was seven years old. I remained here at Castle Idris that spring, and when my father returned in the summer, he brought news of my mother's death. He also brought a new wife, the Lady Mathilda, and her daughter, Gloria."

"Gloria?" the prince asked. "I met no Gloria. Is she here?"

"Yes. She arrived several weeks ago."

"What does she look like?"

"I have not seen her since she returned except at a

distance. She is a rather large person. She was portly even as a child. She is the same age as I, but with black hair, and dark."

"And you grew up together," the prince said.

"No, Your Grace. Gloria was sent to live with the nuns at Eidon. My stepmother lived near there as a child. That was not long after Gloria came to Castle Idris from Wales. Then after my father disappeared, we heard that Gloria had died."

"But she had not died, you say."

"No."

"And she returned to Castle Idris several weeks ago."

"Yes."

"Don't you think that is strange?"

"Yes. I was stunned by the news that she had returned."

"Did you ask about it?" Prince John asked.

"Whom could I ask? We who live at the farm are not permitted in the castle beyond the hinds' hall. And . . . I am not interested in Gloria."

All this time Prince John had been studying me intently. Now he said, "Oh? Why not?"

"Because when Gloria first came to Castle Idris, I was prepared to be her friend, but she was so spiteful and cruel that I soon gave it up and left her alone. Of course she may have changed, but I— I have no contact with her now."

"Does she have heavy, black eyebrows?"

"Yes."

Prince John jumped up, whirled about to face me, and flinging his arms wide apart, he cried, "Then everyone must have known that she was Gloria and not Elaine."

"I do not understand, Your Grace."

"The person I dined with last night was Gloria. She had thick, black eyebrows. She was an enormously corpulent young woman—dark, with black hair. They told me her name was Elaine. But then everyone would have known she was Gloria, not Elaine."

I was amazed. I thought for a moment and then said, "If there was anyone at the castle who was there when Gloria first came, he would know. But there is not anyone left who was there ten years ago. Mathilda has surrounded herself with ladies and gentlemen and knights from Cordal, where she lived with her first husband."

"If all this is true," Prince John said, "Gloria is impersonating you. Don't you care about that?"

"I did not know until now that she was. But could it make any difference?"

Prince John threw himself down beside me again. He seemed unable to remain still for long.

He looked into my eyes and asked, "Why do you say that?"

"Because I no longer have any contact with the people at the castle. As far as they are concerned, I might as well be dead."

"Why has she done this to you?"

"My stepmother? It was not she. She is harmless, silly, almost feebleminded, I think. You must have noticed that. No, it is Sir Tor Malafie, her steward, who is the dangerous one. He has driven many people away, stripped them of their lands, their wealth. It is he who has done this to me."

"What has he done to you, sweet Elaine?"

Prince John was truly interested in me, it seemed, and his smile and gaze were so gentle and kind that I could not refuse to answer his questions. Indeed, I had no wish to refuse.

"Somehow," I said, "Sir Tor persuaded my stepmother to give me to him in marriage. That was when I was seven years old. I refused to marry him. I did not know then that I could refuse, but I was determined to do so. So I was banished from the castle and made the swineherd. It was a punishment. I was to do this until I agreed to marry Sir Tor."

"Poor Elaine. What you must have suffered."

"That first day was the worst. I was permitted to

take only what I could carry in one arm. What would a little girl know about what to take with her? A kitten, a favorite doll, and two small paintings of her mother and father would aid her little in the swineherd's hut. I remember carrying them in one arm, desperately trying to keep the kitten still, while Sir Tor led me from the castle by the other. My eyes were blinded by tears, and I was terrified of what lay in store for me. And then seeing that hut where I was to live, one tiny room of mud and straw, open to the sky in the center of the roof—surely they would not force me to live there, I thought. Fang was there. I was terrified of him and the pigs frightened me. It was more terrible than anything that had ever happened to me."

Fang had begun to growl at the mention of his name, but he ceased when I glared at him.

"You have not agreed to marry Sir Tor, then," Prince John said. "Does he still wish you to?"

"Yes," I replied, "but I shall not."

The prince studied me further for some moments. Then he said, "But how could you have managed them"—he flung his arm toward the pigs—"all alone at seven years of age? How can you manage them now? And where do you eat? How can you live?"

"I eat with the farm workers in the hinds' hall at the castle. It is the old hall. See the tall building just inside the gate?" I gestured toward Castle Idris. "And one lives if one eats and has a place to sleep. I have my staff and knife. They belonged to Ejnar, the old swineherd. He died of fever shortly before I took his place. And I have Fang."

The prince looked at Fang and the dog sullenly returned his gaze.

"He doesn't look like much," Prince John said.

"Half mastiff, half greyhound. We have never been friends. I think he holds me responsible for his master's death somehow. But I do not know what I would have done without him. He works well with the pigs and obeys, though out of training, not out of love for me, certainly.

"And now I have told you all about myself, my lord."

"Then should I tell you something about myself in return?"

I did not reply, but smiled at him.

"There is not much to tell." He jumped up again and stood facing me. "I live at the palace in Tintagal with my father and my younger brother, William, and my sister, Bedraine. My mother is dead. I occupy my time in hunting and hawking, playing chess and backgammon, in singing and dancing. And in tournaments!"

He shouted the word "tournaments," and as he did so, he stretched his arms wide apart and smiled down at me, almost laughing.

"How happy you must be, my lord," I said, returning his smile.

"As happy as you yourself will be one day, sweet maiden. I proclaim it!"

Then with a final wide grin, he flung himself about and ran toward his squire, who waited at the edge of the meadow. The squire saw his master coming and led the prince's horse to him at a trot. Not waiting for the horse to halt, the prince jumped upon the animal, and without looking back at me, he galloped off down the hill so swiftly that the squire was left far behind.

I returned to the same spot the following day. From there I watched the castle gateway for Prince John to come riding out. I knew he would return to see me. I knew, not because of his flowery compliments, but because of what I had seen in his eyes when he had spoken them. There had been gaiety there, certainly— a zest for life, a joy in it—but beneath his exuberance lay something more serious, something important, and I felt it had to do with me. Yes, even though he had been a perfect stranger.

I wanted to see him. I wanted to be with him terribly, to be bathed in the warmth of his kindness and regard. And I wanted to ask him about Gloria; did he know why she used my name?

Someone was riding out of the gateway. But no, it was not Prince John; he would ride a white horse.

Perhaps he would not come. Would he? He must!

Chapter Five

✱✱✱✱✱✱✱✱✱✱✱✱✱✱✱✱✱✱✱✱✱

Gloria's Story

When I arrived at Castle Idris, Mother called me Elaine though my name was Gloria. Above all I wanted to know why she called me that. And I wanted to know why she wanted me with her again.

She had sent me away when I was seven years old, soon after she had married the Duke of Idris. Now I was seventeen. I had not seen the castle since. I had lived with the nuns in Eidon all those years. Mother had grown up near the nunnery and knew of it. It was a cold, dark place. The nuns were appalling women. Their families had cast them out because they were unmarried. They spent their time drinking, eating, and parading about in fancy clothes. When they tired of that, they insulted each other and quarreled.

I loathed them and they ignored me.

I arrived back at Castle Idris in October. My bottom was sore from bumping up and down on a stupid mule for five days. I had been bitten to death by vermin in horrible inns for four nights. I had caught cold. And now my mother did not know my name.

She met me at the entrance to the hall and led me directly to my chamber so that we could talk together privately. We spoke to no one.

I was not glad to see her, though I replied politely to her greetings. Nor was she glad to see me. She had never loved me. She had abandoned me for ten years and had never thought of me once during that time. I hated her for it. I hated the way her lower left leg bent sideways so horribly, causing her to throw herself from side to side to walk. And I detested her mawkish concern for everyone about her, her picky manner, and her stupid absent-mindedness. She repelled me as much now as she had when I was seven years old.

I seemed to repel her equally. She loathed my appearance and even taunted me about it soon after we had arrived in my chamber. I had almost finished eating the bread and cheese, cold chicken, and cake that two gentlewomen had brought me and had drunk most of the wine when she asked me if I intended to eat every morsel and drink every drop. Then she told me that I would become giddy and that obesity was unattractive.

I countered that by saying that lameness was disgusting. I was not going to let the bitch insult me without giving as good as I got. After all, it wasn't my fault that my figure was imposing. I had tried not eating to lose weight, but it had made me sick. I was sensitive about my size, and I hated anyone's mentioning it.

All this made me even more impatient to learn why she did not call me by my name and why she had dragged me to this dismal castle where there was nothing to look at but swamp and ocean.

Finally, after much prodding, she was able to organize her thoughts well enough to tell me that she had spent all of the duke's money. She told me that she had borrowed heavily and that she was now unable to repay the loans. She concluded by saying that she had no idea how this had happened, that she knew nothing about money, had never had to concern

herself with it before, and that she had never known
anything about loans or credit or even that such things
existed.

It was a revolting performance. One would have
thought her demented. I could tell, though, from the
hangings in the rooms we had passed and from Mother's samite gown and the emeralds she wore that what
she had said was true: she had spent freely. She had
always loved the costly and had entertained lavishly.
I could not blame her for that; had she known,
though, that expensive gowns and jewels only made
her face more doglike, she might have shunned them
entirely.

But Mother's scheme of salvation was even more
preposterous than her predicament. At least I thought
so when she told me about it. I laughed aloud and
told her it was absurd. Her plan was this: I was to
impersonate Elaine, my stepsister. Elaine had been
betrothed to the Prince of Tintagal at birth because
my stepfather had saved King Alfred's life during the
Battle of Winchelsea. I was to take Elaine's place and
marry the prince. Mother would then have wealth
aplenty to pay off her debts.

But when I mocked the scheme, I found that my
objections were invalid: Mother told me that the duke
could not identify me because he was dead. Elaine
would not interfere because she did not know she was
betrothed to Prince John—her father had never told
her. Elaine and I would never meet because she had
been banished to the farm as swineherd until she
agreed to marry Sir Tor. So she could not identify me.
After her marriage, of course, she could not marry
anyone else. And no one who had known me when I
was seven years old remained at Castle Idris. Since
then, Mother had surrounded herself with people from
Castle Deleans in Cordal, where she had lived with
her first husband. They would not know me because I
had been a baby when Sir Tor had carried Mother
and me to safety during the siege of the castle that
took my father's life. Finally, though it was well

known that Mother had borne a daughter, she had announced my death shortly after I had left Castle Idris. She had, I was sure, decided to leave me to rot in the convent forever, but then had changed her mind when this present scheme occurred to her.

I had no compunction about impersonating Elaine and marrying Prince John. I had detested the horrid little mouse from the moment I had met her as a child. She had been *so* good, and so thin and pale and dull. Everyone had called her pretty; actually she had been insipid under that snarled mass of pale curls. In contrast, my black hair and flashing eyes were exciting and captivating.

No, Elaine deserved what she got. Let Sir Tor have his reward for saving Mother's and my life, and good riddance. I remembered Sir Tor clearly—he would force Elaine to marry him. He was a persuasive man. I hoped he would beat her. He probably would.

It appeared, then, that I could be accepted as Elaine without question and marry Prince John, and I decided to do so. I would not have long to wait: the ceremony was to take place on John's twentieth birthday. That would be the following January 5.

I realized immediately that I would benefit by such a marriage. Eventually I would become Queen of Tintagal. It was not a very large kingdom. Something bigger would have suited me better, but I supposed Tintagal would have to do.

But I wondered how much my marriage to Prince John would benefit Mother. I surmised she must plan to make appalling demands on the lords of Tintagal to pay for her extravagances, but that would depend upon what kind of man John was, wouldn't it?

Prince John was to visit Castle Idris soon. Mother said that he would come to hunt. But she and I knew that he would come to see his future wife. Until then I should have to endure the monotonous existence in that damp, cold castle.

Two things made those dreary weeks almost endurable: the kitchen and wine cellar were better than I had expected, and I found a pet. I had never liked animals before and they had never liked me. When I first found Aphrodite (that is what I named the cat) asleep on my bed, I thought her a nasty creature. But she was intelligent and admired me immediately. Her silky white hair and violet eyes were lovely. Surely she was the most beautiful cat that had ever lived; so I made her mine and petted her often. Mother hated Aphrodite. She could not understand why I bothered with her. But I knew we suited each other. Her white fur contrasted admirably with my golden skin and black hair.

Chapter Six

✥✥✥✥✥✥✥✥✥✥✥✥✥✥✥✥✥✥

Gloria's Story

Prince John arrived in November. At supper that evening I could tell that Mother was not pleased with him. She did not delay asking about Tintagal, especially about its treasury. It was an embarrassing exhibition: her questions were vague and stupid. But Prince John did not seem to mind. At least he gave no indication that he did.

According to Prince John, his father, King Alfred, was not interested in riches. His health had declined after his return from Palestine, and he simply wished to live the rest of his life quietly and in peace. Mother declared that money in the treasury meant security. Prince John replied that the happiness of his subjects was of prime importance and that he would never demand greater revenues than were necessary to protect the country and support the royal family in quiet dignity.

Clearly Prince John was a stubborn man with a mind of his own. I could see the chests of jewels and

furs Mother had hoped to acquire vanish before her
eyes. No, she was not pleased.

Nor was I. Prince John disliked me immediately. He
had not been able to quell an expression of disgust
when we met. I did not know why he should react that
way—he was as huge a person as I. He was a giant of
a man, but he was all stringy muscle, which I found
just as repellent as he evidently found my fleshiness.
And he was raw and rough-looking with that mass of
unruly hair and thick chin, which his black beard
turned blue.

There could be no bond between myself and such a
man. Before he had spoken four words, I knew that his
only interests would be jousting and swordplay and
hunting and going off to battle.

I had hoped for some polish from the gentleman,
some courtliness. But he ignored me and spoke to me
only when addressed. Well, it did not matter: I would
be his queen whether he liked it or not. It had all been
decided long ago.

Fortunately he was gone all the next day. He had
hunted in the forest, he told us that evening at supper.

During the meal he was unexpectedly attentive to
me. Now he seemed to want to know all about me—
especially where I had lived and what I had done before coming to Castle Idris. He knew I had returned
there three weeks earlier. This surprised me at first.
But then I supposed someone at the castle had told
him about it.

I told him a tale of growing up at the palace of King
Llyr. The king and queen had been friends of my
stepfather, I said, and he wished me to acquire the
proper ladylike graces there. I took care to praise the
elegant, courtly manners of the knights at the palace.
Prince John believed the story, I had thought. But then
his questions took a disturbing direction, and I was not
so sure.

He asked Mother about Gloria. She told John that
Gloria had died during the journey to a nunnery. Then

John asked what she had died of, who was in attendance, and exactly where she had died. He wanted to know all about it. He learned little, though. Mother seemed unable to concentrate on the matter. She was terribly confused, and her answers made no sense at all.

John's questions had made me uneasy, and I was glad when, claiming fatigue, he retired to his chamber directly after supper. And I was glad when he left Castle Idris with his party abruptly the following morning. I hoped I would not see him again until the marriage ceremony.

Not only was I disquieted by Prince John's visit, but another guest provoked me terribly. He was a story-teller—one of those disreputable creatures who travel from castle to castle and live upon the hospitality of hosts. Few travelers stopped at Castle Idris because it was far from well-traveled roads. This was all to the good, of course, since no one was ever turned away without food and lodging and it was grievous to waste either on perfect strangers. Those who had lately found their way to the castle gates had been a dreary handful of pilgrims and clergymen. Since I had arrived, not a player or minstrel or even a poet had appeared to entertain us.

So, though he was almost a dwarf and hideous-looking, this storyteller, Mother and I hoped, might provide us some amusement. After supper he told us several short tales which were mildly humorous, though not worth recounting here.

But then his tone changed, and he told a story which fascinated me, not only because of its content but because I felt that I had heard it before and could not remember it. But the story had an extraordinary effect on Mother. During the telling of it, she stared at the storyteller, her face ashen, her eyes wide, her lips crimped tightly together.

The story was this: Once there lived a powerful sorceress who could put herself anywhere she wished at will. One day she sent herself down into the earth to the Caves of Gold. There she hid herself and watched the Queen of the Caves turn stone into gold. So she learned the secret of how this was done. When the queen discovered that the sorceress knew her secret, she cast a spell which the sorceress was unable to break. Slowly the sorceress herself turned into the purest gold. Then the sorceress's daughter, caring nothing about her mother's memory, melted the body down into gold bars and with this dowry married a wealthy and powerful duke.

The story made Mother angry, and when the storyteller had finished it, she demanded to know where he heard such an absurd tale. And she berated him for wasting her time with drivel.

I could not understand why she had become angry over a story, but I thought no more about it then because the storyteller presented me with a riddle. It was this: A woodcutter and his wife had a child. When the baby was born, a fairy appeared and told them that because they were such good people, they might choose any three of nine gifts for their son. The gifts were a winged horse, a cane, one hundred books, laughter, an orb and scepter, a harp, a sword, gold, and a heart. Which gifts did the woodcutter and his wife choose?

I was puzzled about the last gift, and I asked what the storyteller meant. He said the gift was a human heart. I thought this grotesque and told him so.

The answer to the riddle was obvious. I declared that the three proper gifts were the orb and scepter because then the boy would be a king, the gold because he would then be wealthy and could buy anything he wanted, and the sword, with which he could slay his enemies.

But when I asked if my answer was correct, the storyteller told me there was no correct answer, any more than there was a correct story. I did not know what he meant by that, but I knew I had been tricked. I left the room immediately. But before I walked through the doorway, I paused and sniffed in disgust at the little hypocrite.

The experience had left me strangely disturbed, but that had been only the beginning of an anxious night. Aphrodite would provide far pleasanter company than anyone else, I decided. So I went up to my chamber, where I found her sleeping on my bed. But she was petulant and did not want to be disturbed. When I picked her up and began to pet her, she leaped away from me and left the room by the window and the adjoining roof. This left me standing at the window looking out at the empty sea, which was hardly captivating or exciting.

I wished then that something, anything, would happen to relieve the boredom. My wish was granted by a knock on my chamber door. "Enter," I called.

The door opened slowly and there on the threshold stood the Duke of Idris. It had been ten years since I had seen my stepfather, but I recognized him immediately. He had not changed at all.

He stood there without speaking and I did the same. I was too astonished, seeing him appear like that, to do anything else. After my initial surprise, I remembered that Mother had said he was dead. I drew back, suddenly afraid.

He asked, "Do you know me?"

"Yes," I said. "You are my stepfather, but I thought you were dead."

It was then that the strangest thing happened: without another word my stepfather turned from me and walked away down the corridor. I thought now that I would never marry Prince John—that the duke would expose me. I ran out of the room after him, but I could not see him, nor could I hear him. The corridor was empty and still.

I turned and ran in the opposite direction down to the hall and Mother. She was not there, but I found her in her chamber. When I told her about my experience, she did not believe that I had seen the duke. All my insistence that I had could not convince her. It was impossible, she kept saying. Then when I tried to convince her still further and declared that our plan was ruined, she became annoyed, said that she had a headache, and asked me to leave her.

How could she be so certain that the duke was dead? How could she be so sure that I had not seen him, when I had?

Chapter Seven

❋❋❋❋❋❋❋❋❋❋❋❋❋❋❋❋❋❋❋❋❋

Elaine's Story

He did not keep me waiting long. Very soon, as I sat on the hillside watching for him to appear, he rode out of the castle gateway on his white horse. But he rode with his entire party, in the midst of his noble attendants. Behind him came the pack horses, fully laden. Prince John, then, was leaving.

As I watched the procession approach, I wondered why he was leaving so soon. Surely he had not come all the way from Tintagal to visit Castle Idris for only two days. He would not come to see me any more, then. Yes, I had dreamed of that—of the joy we would share in being together. But now he was going away and I would never see him again.

I watched him eagerly as he approached, memorizing the way he sat on his horse. I wanted to memorize his face, but he was too far away for that. And he was too far away for me to be sure of his expression when he looked up at me as he passed. I thought I saw longing there, as if he wished to leave his companions and ride up the hill to me, but I probably imagined it. I wanted him to come and say goodbye, and to say that he would return.

He remained gazing in my direction for almost a minute as he rode by, but he did not leave the procession. Instead, he looked away from me finally, and rode on.

He was gone. I listened intently until the distant hum of the horses' hoofs had vanished, and then I lectured myself aloud: "What did you expect? That Prince John of Tintagal would fall in love with Elaine the swineherd? Do you think he believed you are the Lady Elaine? No, how could you expect him to? He would have come to say goodbye if he had. No, he thought you an imaginative fool—amusing for a few minutes, but then to be forgotten. Forget him, Elaine. Take care of your pigs. At least your life is your own here in the woods and fields. At least you have that."

But I could not forget Prince John—his eyes, his smile, the way his athletic body moved. And though the sun shone, the day was dark for me, and though the sky was autumn blue, it was gray to me. And it seemed forever before it was time to go back to the farm for the night.

Chapter Eight

✳✳✳✳✳✳✳✳✳✳✳✳✳✳✳✳✳✳✳✳

Elaine's Story

Many afternoons later, as Fang and I drove the pigs toward the farm, I saw a man sitting on the parapet of one of the stone bridges that crossed the marsh inlets below the castle. He must be a pilgrim, I thought, on his way to spend the night at the castle. He had paused there to rest before walking on up the hill to the gateway.

Ordinarily I would not have paid attention to the man; it was not unusual to pass visitors on the road. But he seemed to be watching me intently. This drew my attention to him, and I noticed that unlike most travelers, he carried no staff or belongings. His cloak was of plain lightweight wool—much too light a fabric for late autumn, I thought. He wore no hat, and instead of heavy boots, he wore thin sandals, which exposed his feet.

As I drew abreast of him, I nodded and smiled. And as I did so, I noticed that his sandals and feet were clean—not covered with dirt and dust as I had expected. He was an old man with a broken nose.

Shrewd eyes glinted at me beneath long yellow-gray hair. A full, untrimmed yellow-gray beard hung to his chest.

He was small—almost a dwarf. I noticed this particularly because as I gazed at him, he fell, rather than jumped, to the ground from his perch, even though the wall reached only to my shoulder. I ran to him at once to help, wondering how he had gotten up there in the first place, but he had picked himself up from the ground with surprising agility before I reached him.

"Did you hurt yourself?" I asked.

"Of course not!" he said. "I never hurt myself. You are Elaine the swineherd?"

"Yes," I replied. "How did you know?"

He pointed with his arm and with his center two fingers, which he held together oddly, to my pigs. "Unless I am mistaken, those animals are swine," he said. His eyes twinkled. "And unless I am mistaken again, that sow is about to bathe in the marsh."

I ran to the pig and with my staff prodded her back onto the bridge, where Fang herded her to join the others.

"Thank you," I said to the little man. "If she had gotten into the mud, it would not have been easy to get her out."

"I shall walk along with you, then," the man said, "and I shall tell you a riddle as we go."

"Very well," I said. "I like riddles." The man's eyes smiled at me and I returned his smile. "But I have nothing to give you in return."

He motioned my objection aside and said, "A woodcutter and his wife had a child. When the baby was born, a fairy appeared and told them that because they were such good people, they might choose any three of nine gifts for their son. The gifts were a winged horse, a cane, one hundred books, laughter, an orb and scepter, a harp, a sword, gold, and a heart. Which gifts did the woodcutter and his wife choose?"

"What kind of heart was it?" I asked.

"A human heart," the man replied.

"Was it a man's heart or a woman's?"

"A woman's." His eyes glinted.

"Then I would say they chose the heart," I said, smiling down at him again. "Because I think the most precious gift a man can receive is a woman's heart. Without love, life would be empty, don't you agree? And then I think they chose the cane. After all, the boy would have no use for it until he was an old man. That would mean he would have a long life. And— I wish he could have had more gifts. I wish he could have traveled on the winged horse. And I wish he could have had music and knowledge. But I think joy is more important than any of those. So I would say they chose the heart, the cane, and laughter."

We walked on then in silence as I thought about the riddle. All the while, I think, the man studied me.

Finally I said, "But that is not really a riddle, is it? Everyone would have a different answer, wouldn't he? According to what he thought was important. So there couldn't be any right answer, could there?"

The man grinned at me. I could tell that he did so even under all that hair.

By that time we had reached the fork in the road. "I must leave you now," I said. "That is the way to the castle. I go this way to the farm."

I left him, calling to Fang and pointing to a pig who had decided to follow the pilgrim. Fang turned the animal in the right direction, and we proceeded to the farm.

Shortly I looked back and saw the man walking toward the distant gate. But then when I looked a second time, he was gone. He must have walked very fast to have gotten through the gateway in such a terribly short time, I thought.

But that evening stranger things were yet to happen.

Chapter Nine

✳✳✳✳✳✳✳✳✳✳✳✳✳✳✳✳✳✳✳

Elaine's Story

Brian and Gueneth asked me to walk back to the farm with them after supper that evening. Ordinarily I walked alone. This was not because I disliked their company; I had come to love them both. But I had told them that I preferred walking alone so as not to provoke gossip or arouse suspicion among others at the farm. The laborers feared Sir Tor and anyone connected with the castle, so they had mistrusted me from the beginning. And I had not wanted their mistrust to spread to Brian and Gueneth because of me.

I had passed through the gateway and had paused to gaze at the sunset—thousands of flaming orange-pink cloudlets crowded in an aquamarine sky.

"Elaine," Gueneth called. "Come, walk down with us." When I had joined her and Brian, she continued: "You looked so sad, standing there all alone. What were you thinking about, my dear?"

"The sunset," I replied. "And a pilgrim who told me a riddle this afternoon."

I had been thinking about the pilgrim, but not as

much as about Prince John, though I would not tell
Brian and Gueneth that.

I told them about the riddle then and about the
strange little man who had told it to me. And then
we talked about other things, and I asked if there
had been any news of Prince John.

"Where is Tintagal?" I asked Brian.

"Far to the west," he said. "Across the land to the
sea that washes on the Irish shores."

"Is it *very* far?"

"Yes." He grinned at me. "Why do you ask? Are
you planning to go there?"

"I? Oh, no! I was just wondering."

"I am glad to hear it. It is a long way and dangerous. Beyond the great forest here"—he gestured
to the wooded hills west of the castle—"lie the plains
of Mortmoor. The mists come down in a moment
there, and one can step off the road and lose his way
among the bogs and quicksands. Great packs of
wolves roam the place. No one lost on the moors at
night lives to see the dawn, they say. Beyond that lies
another great wood where a dragon lives. It is said
that the trees are burned to black stumps for miles
around his lair. And then there are the high mountains
to cross. A giant lives in them somewhere. It is said
he can smell a man from miles away."

"Why should he do that?" I asked. "What would
he do then?"

"Catch him and eat him."

"Eat a human being?" I shuddered.

"When he can get one. If not, a farmer's cow or
sheep will do—anything with blood in its veins. No
one has lived anywhere near the giant for a long
time, but they still say he will travel great distances
when he is hungry. A man would have to know the
way if he wanted to go to Tintagal."

By this time we had reached the smithy. The sun
had gone, carrying its brilliant colors away with it.
Brian and Gueneth climbed the stairs to their room
above the forge. I took Fang his supper, and then re-

turned to the smithy, fetched my pallet from the corner of the room, unrolled it before the fire, removed my belt and knife and set them on the ground beside the mattress, then sat down to watch the tiny flames that leaped now and then from the banked coals.

I thought about Prince John. I must have sunk deep into my reverie because without a sound or warning of any kind, a voice from behind me said, "Elaine?"

I thought it was Sir Tor. I turned, a shiver of fear running down my spine, to see who had spoken.

"Elaine?" he said. "Don't you know me?"

I jumped up then and ran to the man. "Father?" I cried. *"Father?"* I threw my arms about him and hugged him to me. "Oh, Father, Father. Where have you been? Where have you *been?"*

I was crying. I drew back a little to look at him. Though the light was dim and my tears blurred my sight, I could see that he had not changed.

"Dearest, dearest Father," I cried, hugging him again. "I knew you would come. I knew you would. Are you all right? What happened? Where did you go? Why did you leave me?"

But instead of answering my questions, Father grasped my arms, pushed me away from him, and said in a voice that sounded strange to me, "I cannot stay. I must go."

"Go?" I asked. "But you have just come. You cannot go. We have not . . . "

As I spoke, Father opened the door and stepped out into the night. I ran after him at once. I looked all about the yard, but it was empty. He was gone.

I wondered later as I lay on my mattress before the fire how he could have vanished so quickly. Surely I would have seen him walk away. The yard outside the forge was of hard-packed earth—wide and empty. There was no place to hide there. I should have seen him walking away and heard his footsteps. But I had seen no one and the air itself had been still.

How could he have vanished so quickly? How

strange that I had not heard him arrive. I should have heard the door open. Had it been Father, then, or had it been his spirit? No, it had been he in the flesh; I was sure of that. I had felt his body as I had hugged him. He had been real. He must have had some reason for leaving like that; he would not have left me if he could have stayed.

Above all these thoughts my mind kept saying, "He is alive." Over and over, "He is alive. He is alive. He is alive."

I slept at last—a joyous sleep. Father was alive, and he would return and take me away from all this misery.

When the door to the forge opened early the following morning, I thought at once that he had come for me. But it was not Father who stepped into the room.

Chapter Ten

✖✖✖✖✖✖✖✖✖✖✖✖✖✖✖✖✖✖✖✖

Elaine's Story

It was Sir Tor.

"Ah, my little dove is awake," he said.

"What is it, Sir Tor?" I asked. "I have just risen. I have not yet washed. Why do you come here at this hour?"

He walked to me, saying, "It is never too early for lovers. Give me a kiss."

He grabbed me, pulled me to him and kissed me on the mouth. I did not resist him, but held myself rigid and unyielding.

"Cold as the morning air," Sir Tor grumbled, releasing me. "Can't you put some warmth into your kisses? I'll teach you how."

He grasped my arms and pulled me to him. But before he could kiss me, I said, "I have just wakened, Sir Tor, and I am not in the mood for games. And I cannot believe that you have gotten out of a warm bed to come here for that reason yourself."

He let go of me with a snarl. "I've a good mind to show you how warm my bed is, little one."

"Why do you say that to me? You have never spoken like that before. You have always been a gentleman. You have always been kind. Why do you threaten me now?"

"Because I long for you," he cried. "I long to have you in my bed, as my wife." Now he pulled me gently to him. "Please, Elaine. Please, little one. I will be good to you. I will give you everything I have. Marry me! Come to understand me. Come to love me."

"Is that why you came? To ask me to marry you?"

"The Lady Mathilda wants to see you. She sent me to bring you to the castle."

I was too surprised by this news to speak.

"Why does she want to see you?" Sir Tor asked. "What were you doing while I was away?"

"I do not know," I said. "Nothing! I did not know you were away."

"You must have done something." Sir Tor examined me through narrowed eyes. His fingers tightened on my arm.

"No! What could I have done? Why should she wish to see me? I have not seen her for years. You must know that."

Sir Tor began to pull me toward the door. I told him that he might at least allow me to wash my face. He did, and after I had put on the cloak he had given me, we walked together up the hill to the castle.

The sun had risen above the sea in a chill, pale sky. It cast our shadows, long and thin, across the road. We did not speak. At first Sir Tor clutched my arm, but I shrugged him off, thinking about that morning long ago when he had led me away from my home by the hand. Now after ten years I would pass through the great hall again.

Would I remember it? Would it have changed? I remembered it well. And as Sir Tor led me through the hall, I saw that it had indeed changed. Some of the windows were now of colored glass, and hangings covered the walls. They pictured scenes of battle and the hunt in brilliant blues, greens and crimsons. Flowers, birds, trees, horses, knights in armor, banners and shields of all designs and colors blazed from the walls.

Even the Great Staircase and Great Chamber were hung with tapestries. After we had passed through the Great Chamber, we climbed the north staircase and walked down the long open gallery where I had spent so many afternoons as a child waiting for a ship to sail by on the sea. Finally we paused outside a chamber which had once been my mother's and had then become my stepmother's.

Sir Tor told me to go in. I knocked on the door, opened it, and stepped into the room. Sir Tor did not follow me. My stepmother was not there. I was alone.

When Mother had occupied the room, its stone walls and floor had been unadorned. But now embroidered white swans swam among golden reeds on crimson wall hangings. Even the floor was covered with tapestries. Mother's bed lay swathed in scarlet velvet embroidered with the Idris badge.

All this luxury amazed me. I stood gazing about the room for several moments. Then I crossed it to the window to look into the courtyard garden below. There on the rim of the fish pool sat my stepmother. She stared down into the water almost as in a trance.

I went out to her, and as I approached, I said, "Stepmother? Did you wish to see me?"

She looked up, startled, and then, her face puckering with intense emotion, she said, "Elaine! My *dear* child." She held out her hand, her straight fingers pressed tightly together in a clump. "How marvelous to see you. Thank you for coming all this way to see me. Sit down—here beside me. Isn't it delightful in the sun and out of the wind?"

I sat down beside her on the pool's rim, and we examined each other.

"You look so *well*, Elaine," she said.

"And so do you, Stepmother," I said.

"The life out-of-doors in our lovely countryside seems to have agreed with you."

"I have been well, thank you."

"If only your father could see you now."

I did not reply.

"How proud he would be."

Still I said nothing.

"His death was such a dreadful blow to us all. How I miss him. You must miss him too. Death is so final—never to hear his voice. Never to see our loved one again. He is so irrevocably gone. Dead."

"But he is not!" I said.

"Not?" She gazed at me with round, bewildered eyes.

"No! He is alive. He came to me last night. He asked me if I knew him. Of *course* I knew him."

"A dream—an apparition of the mind."

"No, Stepmother. I did not imagine it. I felt him. I clasped him in my arms. He was *real!*"

"Did he speak? What did he say?"

"He asked if I knew him. And then when I put my arms about him, he said he must go, and he left me. Did you see him?"

"No, my dear. You were dreaming."

"No, it was no dream."

"Well—perhaps. We shall have to wait and see."

"He will put it all right now."

" 'Put it right'?" Stepmother asked.

"He would not wish me to marry Sir Tor. And I shall soon return to the castle to live."

"We should *love* that, my dear," Stepmother simpered. "It was only for your own good, you know. Sir Tor is a wonderful man. I would trust him with my life. Elaine, my dear, he would make a superb husband. And he is so *captivated* by you. He would do *anything* for you."

"I shall never marry him," I said.

"You must not be hasty. Marriage is too important for that. Sir Tor is such an excellent man. He would take good—"

"I shall never marry him."

"We shall see," she said, standing up.

I stood too. "How is Gloria?" I asked.

My stepmother did not answer me. Instead she turned from me and began to walk toward the steps to her chamber.

"Or do you call her Elaine now?"

She looked at me then, annoyed. "Elaine?" she said.

"Yes. I understand she calls herself Elaine. Is that so, Stepmother?"

"Whatever gave you that idea?"

"Prince John told me that Gloria pretends to be the Lady Elaine, daughter of the Duke of Idris. Of course I told him who she really is. Why? Why does she do this?"

Stepmother came to me then, linked her arm in mine, and began to propel me toward her chamber. "Silly man," she said, smiling at me. "Such a silly man. Not an ounce of intelligence. And off hawking and hunting all day. How they can do it is beyond me. Blood, I suppose. They like to see blood. *We* are so fortunate, you and—"

"Why does Gloria impersonate me, Stepmother?"

"Impersonate you? My dear, what nonsense. Gloria is *sensitive*. Such a sensitive child. She hated to leave Castle Idris. You remained, but she had to go. It was for her own good, of course. The nuns taught her more than she could ever have learned here. Such dedicated women."

And she went on to tell me about the nuns, having forgotten entirely about my question. Surely she was in her dotage. I did not ask about Gloria again. I knew it would be useless.

Our progress was slow because of my stepmother's limp, but we finally climbed to the gallery and entered her chamber.

Once inside, she said, "Now we will have something to revive us."

She left me then, hobbled into an adjoining room, and presently returned carrying two glasses of wine.

"Sit here with me," she said, walking to a table separating two chairs. She set the glasses down on the table, and we sat opposite each other.

She sipped from her glass. "There is nothing like a little wine to refresh the spirits," she said. "Come, come. Drink."

I reached for the glass before me, but it moved away from my fingers. I reached for it again. Again it moved away from me of its own accord. I looked at Stepmother to see if she noticed. She gazed at my face, smiling. Now I reached quickly for my glass, but before I could grasp it, it slid to the table's edge and fell to the floor, spilling the wine on the carpet and spattering my stepmother's silken gown.

"Clumsy!" Stepmother cried, jumping up. "Clumsy dolt!" She whisked a handkerchief from her sleeve and blotted the spots on her skirt. "Go!" She pointed imperiously to the door between dabs. "Go! Go! Go!"

I ran from the room, closing the door tightly behind me. Then I ran without pausing through the corridors and down the staircase to the hall.

Sir Tor stood in the hall. As I ran past him he reached out and caught my arm.

Chapter Eleven

✱✱✱✱✱✱✱✱✱✱✱✱✱✱✱✱✱✱✱✱

Elaine's Story

"What did she want?" Sir Tor growled.

"I don't know," I cried, trying to wrench myself free of him. "She did not tell me what she wanted. I spilt some wine on her dress, and she was furious. Let go of me! I don't know!"

He let me go then and I ran across the room. At the doorway I glanced back at Sir Tor. He had swung about and now hurried toward the Grand Staircase and my stepmother's room.

It was only later, when I had driven the pigs into the woods, that I could think clearly about what had happened at the castle. I had been afraid that in my stepmother's fury over her gown she would send Sir Tor to punish me.

But now that I sat on a fallen tree in the woods, I felt hidden and safe for the present. Why had my stepmother asked me to the castle? There seemed no purpose in her having done so.

Above all the incident of the wineglass puzzled me. The glass had seemed alive. It had not wanted to be grasped. Had my stepmother watched it move? Was the glass bewitched? I could not explain what had happened. But I shuddered as again in my mind I saw the glass slide of its own accord across the table, topple over the edge of it, and tumble to the floor.

That evening as I sat in the smithy on my mattress looking into the fire, as had become my custom before lying down to sleep, the door opened. Again I thought for a moment that Father had returned; again it was Sir Tor. Somehow I felt that he had watched the smithy until Brian had gone upstairs to Gueneth and I had had time to settle myself for the night. How else could he have timed his arrival so perfectly to find me alone, yet not asleep?

"What do you want?" I asked.

Sir Tor did not speak. He walked to where I sat and stood above me, gazing calmly down at my face.

"What is it, Sir Tor?" I asked. "I am about to go to sleep."

Sir Tor's mouth curled in a twisted smile, and he grunted.

"I— Did you find out what Stepmother wanted?" I asked.

"Aye," he said.

"What?"

"You to marry me."

"I told her I cannot."

Then Sir Tor grasped the neck of my kirtle and pulled me to my feet. He locked an arm about me and fastened his lips upon mine. I fought him, but the more I struggled, the tighter he held me. And all the while his kiss defiled my mouth.

I felt his debauched readiness, and it terrified me. I stopped struggling and endured the assault, holding my breath and praying that he would finish soon.

At last he released my mouth and I breathed again. But he did not speak. He stared at me, gauging my

reactions to what he had done and smiling that twisted
grin.

"Let me go," I said.

He held me tighter.

"You are hurting me."

Still he said nothing. His eyes frightened me.

"What are you going to do?"

His answer was to sink to the ground, pulling me
onto my pallet with him. With one hand he restrained
me. With the other he grasped the neck of my kirtle
and smock and tore them from me, exposing my body.
His mouth and hand befouled my pure breasts and
loins. Then he fell heavily upon me. I writhed and
struck at him, trying to free myself. I screamed. He
clapped a hand over my mouth. His other prepared
his invasion.

My knife lay on the ground beside the mattress. I
grasped it tightly, drew it from its scabbard, and with
a might born of fear and disgust, plunged its blade
deep into Sir Tor's back.

He howled with pain. He flung himself away from
me and wailed horribly as he crawled beyond my
reach. Sitting up and glaring at me, unable to believe
what I had done, he felt for the knife handle. With a
terrible gasp he pulled the blade from his shoulder.
Blood spurted from the wound. At once his tunic was
red with it.

"Pig!" I hissed, pulling a sheepskin in front of me.
"Foul, ugly beast! Filthy, stinking old man!"

Sir Tor sat gaping at me, his hand still clutching my
bloody knife in his lap. His eyes slowly narrowed to
slits, his jaw clenched, and tossing my knife aside, he
staggered to his feet. He stood there for a moment,
staring at me with an expression of such malevolent
hatred that it turned my blood cold.

Then he lunged at me. I leaped to my feet; Brian
and Gueneth burst into the room; and Sir Tor fell
senseless to the ground before me.

"I've killed him," I said calmly to Gueneth and

Brian. "He tried to— He attacked me and I killed him."

Looking down at Sir Tor and the blood that soaked his tunic and flowed onto the ground, I suddenly felt sick. And only then, fully realizing what I had done, I felt terrified.

I dashed to Gueneth and threw my arms around her. "What will they do to me?" I cried. "I've killed him. What will they do?"

Gueneth held me and together we watched Brian. He ran to Sir Tor's body and knelt beside it. With amazing speed, he tore Sir Tor's bloody tunic and shirt off him, stood, shed his own shirt, ripped a piece of fabric from it, wadded it, and thrust the wad against the wound in Sir Tor's shoulder. He called for Gueneth to help him.

Gueneth held the pad in place while Brian tore the remainder of his shirt into strips. Working together frantically, Brian held Sir Tor's torso off the ground and pressed the pad against the wound while Gueneth wound the strips of fabric tightly over it and around Sir Tor's chest and shoulder. Finally she knotted two ends of the bandage, and it was done.

"Go and put something on, Brian," she said to her husband. She came to me and wrapped her arms around me. "He is not dead. Thank God! He is not dead."

Then Gueneth got my cloak, took the sheepskin from me, and wrapped the cloak about me. We stood holding each other, gazing at Sir Tor's bandaged body, and hardly speaking until Brian returned. He was fully dressed.

"I'll go and get Borel and Chedric," he said to Gueneth. "And the cart. We'll take him up to the castle."

"What will you say?" Gueneth asked.

"I'll— That I found him. That he crawled in here for help."

"But he will tell them what happened."

"If he ever talks again. If not, well . . . " Looking at me, Brian added quickly, "He will live. It would take more than that to kill him. And— he won't tell. He won't let them know a woman did it." Turning back to Gueneth, he said, "Take her upstairs with you. Keep her with you tonight. I will go and get the cart."

I spent that night with Gueneth. She comforted me as best she could, but finally she fell asleep. After that I lay wide awake feeling terribly alone and frightened. What would Sir Tor do to me if he lived?

In the morning, Brian told us that he had still been alive when he had left Sir Tor at the castle. My stepmother had been called, and she had taken charge of him. And when Sir Tor was still alive that next night and had eaten a plate of soup a day later, we felt certain that he would survive.

I heard nothing from my stepmother—nothing from the castle. Everything went on at the farm as though nothing had happened. No one there believed the story that Sir Tor had been wounded in a fight with a nameless assassin and had crawled to the smithy for help, as Brian told them. Everyone knew perfectly well that I slept there on winter nights and that Sir Tor coveted me. But they were so terrified of Sir Tor that his injury was never spoken of—at least not within my hearing, or Brian's or Gueneth's, either.

And I heard nothing from Sir Tor, which frightened me most. I could not forget the look of murderous hatred I had seen in his eyes, and I knew that he would have his revenge upon me. So I decided to run away. But I had nowhere to go, no one to run to. Brian and Gueneth convinced me that it would be more dangerous to run off into the woods than to remain where they could help me if need be.

I agreed and remained at the farm, caring for the pigs as usual and waiting. Since Brian had arranged a lock on the door, I slept safely enough at the forge at night. And I always told him where I would be during the day so that he could ride out if possible to be sure I was all right. But the suspense was intolerable. Neither Brian or Gueneth nor I knew what we waited for, when it would come, or how to prepare for it.

So, many days later when I saw Sir Tor ride through the woods toward me, I felt almost a sense of relief.

Chapter Twelve

****

Elaine's Story

I would know now what lay in store for me. It was very early in the morning. The pigs were foraging for their breakfast. Fang had curled up in the sun and lay dozing. Sir Tor rode a hackney and led a mule by a rope.

I stood and faced him as he reined his horse to a halt before me. Fang growled almost inaudibly, but he did not move. Sir Tor ignored him.

"You are to come with me," Sir Tor said.

He did not speak angrily. But there was a cold, controlled, almost smug detachment about his manner which I had never encountered before. It puzzled me.

"Now?" I replied. "What of the pigs?"

"They will be looked after."

"Where are you taking me?"

"The Lady Mathilda does not want you here. I am taking you to the nunnery at Eidon."

I thought quickly. So I was to be placed in a nun-

nery. This was far better than anything I had antici-
pated.

"But that is several days' journey."

Sir Tor did not reply, but gazed impassively down
at me.

"I must go and get my things."

"You will come now. The smith will keep them for
you."

"No! I want to tell them where I have gone and to
say goodbye. There are some things I must take with
me. I cannot go off like this without notice. No! We
will go tomorrow."

Sir Tor dismounted. He did not hurry. With a ghost
of a smile, holding the reins of his horse and the mule
in his left hand, he stepped before me. With his right
hand he struck me across the face.

I staggered backward from the force of the blow.
My face felt on fire. But it was the lack of emotion in
Sir Tor's attack that terrified me. I knew that if I
provoked him, he would beat me, possibly to death,
without the slightest remorse. Any affection or regard
that he may have felt for me had vanished.

With his eyes, Sir Tor directed me to the mule. I
walked to it without further objection and mounted.
Sir Tor climbed into the saddle, grimacing with pain
as he did so. Then we rode off, Sir Tor leading my
mule by the rope.

We rode not through the village but around it on
unfrequented paths. Then somewhere beyond it we
joined a main road which wound westward.

Sir Tor and I had not spoken since we had left Fang
and the pigs. Finally, after we had ridden for perhaps
an hour, I called to him: "You may take the lead off
the mule, Sir Tor. You will only tire yourself and the
mule too. I will not run away, if that is what you are
afraid of."

Sir Tor waited for me to catch up to him. He un-
tied the mule, wrapped the rope about his waist and
tied it there. Then, without speaking to me, he rode
on. And I followed him.

We rode all day, stopping only once to drink at a wayside spring. The road wound constantly upward, and during the early afternoon the forest shrank to low shrubs and finally disappeared altogether. Now we rode across a great, heaving plain—an ocean of grassy waves breaking against jagged stone peaks. Now and then a dusting of fresh snow blew across the dun grass. The sky was the color of lead.

On and on we rode across that endless moor. And hour after hour it looked the same. Where would we spend the night in that forsaken place? I wondered. Sir Tor hunched in the saddle; his shoulder pained him. Surely we must stop soon. The sun set and it grew cold.

Finally we left the road and followed a faint track. Soon the track disappeared entirely, and I wondered how Sir Tor could find the way. It was shortly after that that we descended into a little valley ringed by low hills.

Here Sir Tor reined his horse to a halt, and I drew my mule up beside him.

"Can you find the way?" I asked him.

He did not reply. Instead he removed the rope from around his waist, and without dismounting, retied it to the mule's bridle. He would lead me now, I thought, so that we would not lose each other in the waning light.

Sir Tor moved closer beside me. Then, with that same glare of malevolent hatred that I had seen the night I had stabbed him, he flung his right fist across my face, knocked me out of the saddle, and sent me crashing to the ground.

Immediately, without looking at me again, he spurred his horse forward and shot up the hill, pulling the mule behind him. In a moment he reached the brow and sank from sight down the other side.

I scrambled to my feet and ran after him, but by the time I reached the hilltop, he was gone. Before me lay another deserted hill, and lying beyond that yet another, and another, and another. I watched to see which direction Sir Tor had taken, but I did not see him again.

I soon realized that I must find my own way back to the road. First I must find the track that we had taken. I thought I remembered the knoll to my left and ran to it. The track lay on the other side of it, I decided. But when I climbed to the crest, I looked down a slope I did not recognize. It was growing dark now. I ran down the slope toward a rocky hillock, but even as I did so I knew I would never find the path. I was lost.

I stopped to catch my breath, holding myself tense, willing myself not to panic. I must be calm. I must find a cave or hollow in which to spend the night.

Father! I cried in my thoughts. If you are a spirit, come to me now. Help me! I looked up desperately, hoping that he might appear on the hill before me. As I gazed up at it, something rose into view.

It was a figure, but it was not the figure of a man.

Chapter Thirteen

✱✱✱✱✱✱✱✱✱✱✱✱✱✱✱✱✱✱✱✱

Gloria's Story

I began to wonder if the duke might have appeared to me not in the flesh, but in the spirit. I wanted to know if this was so. If the spirit of my stepfather was to haunt me at any time of the day or night, I wanted to prepare myself for it. And I wanted to find a way of exorcising him from my presence. As the night progressed, the thought terrified me more and more. Lying in bed, I drew the covers over my head, curled up in a ball under them, and prayed that the spirit would not return. It was a long time before I was able to sleep.

In the morning I was more rational and decided to find out more about the duke's death. I had slept late, and when I went in search of Mother, I was not surprised to find that she had left her bower and now sat in the courtyard garden nearest her chamber. She sat wrapped in a heavy cloak, on the rim of the fish pool, staring into its depths.

I went out to her, but she was not glad to see me. I could tell she wished to be alone. I thought she might at least prefer her daughter's company over that of the fishes, and told her so. She replied that it was no time to be tiresome, and we quarreled.

When we tired of baiting each other, I asked if my stepfather had cared to appear to her as yet. I was amazed when she told me I had not seen the duke the night before, but that I had seen either his spirit or someone impersonating him. Then she said that her husband was dead, that she had been with him when he had died. She was certain, however, that I had seen somebody who looked like my stepfather. She had discovered that Elaine had seen what she thought was her father the night before. Mother had, it turned out, summoned Elaine to the castle early that morning, and Elaine had told her about it.

But when I asked Mother what it meant, she became angry and told me to go away, that she wanted to think, and that the pool would soon be frozen over with ice.

Clearly her mind was wandering again, so I left her sitting on the pool's rim, staring at the fishes. She remained sitting that way until suppertime. And when I found her there again, staring into the water the next morning, I began to wonder what she saw in it. I watched and waited until she came indoors, and then ran into the garden and sat on the rim of the pool just as she had done. But I saw only reflected sky in the water and carp swimming in its murky depths.

Mother returned to the garden while I was sitting there, and asked what I was doing. I told her that I had been doing just what she had done for the past two days and that I hoped it had helped her—it had done nothing for me. She retorted that looking into the water calmed her nerves, and if I used my mind instead of playing games, I might have a better understanding of what was going on around me. And what, I asked, had been going on around me that I did not understand any better than she did?

Mother told me the following things: The name of

the storyteller who had distressed me so was Merlin. I had never heard of Merlin, and asked who he was. Mother said he was a powerful magician, and that it must have been he who had appeared to me and Elaine in the guise of the Duke of Idris. Merlin had come magically to the castle. He had not been seen entering the gate or leaving it. He had assumed the appearance of the duke and appeared to me and Elaine in order to determine who was the duke's rightful daughter. I asked Mother why he would possibly be interested in Elaine and me and how she had learned these things. She mumbled something then about the Lady Eustace having recognized Merlin. She said it could not make the slightest difference what Merlin had decided as a result of his masquerade.

It seemed to me that if it made no difference, Merlin would not have masqueraded in the first place, and I told Mother that. Then she described her dream to me. The dream was so real, she said, that it was more than a dream: it was a prophecy.

She had dreamed that it was written in a great book that two maidens would each claim to be the Duke of Idris' daughter. The one presenting King Alfred of Tintagal with the finest dowry would become the Princess Elaine.

At this I lost patience with Mother entirely. I told her that relying on dreams was ridiculous. And even if the dream was true, how could a swineherd acquire a dowry other than pigs' droppings? It was all too absurd. Her imaginings were making me nervous. We should have done something practical.

Mother sneered and asked what that could have been.

I said that we should have found out more about this Merlin or whoever he was while he was here. We should have sent a woman to his bed. A pretty woman could get anything she wanted from a man.

After I had imparted this wisdom to Mother, I left her and went to my room, where Aphrodite waited eagerly for my attentions. The exquisite animal was extraordinarily discerning: she worshiped me. But she might have been more considerate: so often she did not appear when I wanted her.

For instance, the following day I searched everywhere for Aphrodite and asked everyone I saw where she was. But I could not find her. Finally in desperation I went to Mother's chamber to ask if she had seen my cat.

Mother was not alone. She stood talking to another woman. The woman stood with her back to me. She was dressed in a velvet gown trimmed with fur. The woman's silky white hair was elaborately arranged in a net of pearls. Because of her hair, I thought she must be old. But when she turned around to look at me, I discovered that she was young. She was the most beautiful maiden I had ever seen. She left us then without saying a word. And as she swept by, she gazed at me in a strangely smug way with lovely almond-shaped violet eyes.

I shivered, frightened by a nameless feeling. I asked Mother who the woman was. Mother told me that her name was Bellezza. She was the daughter of Lady Eustace from Castle Deleans, who had come to visit Mother. She and her mother were leaving the castle that morning for Orkney, and she had wanted to pay her respects to Mother before she left.

I never saw the woman at Castle Idris again, nor Aphrodite, either.

For many days Mother was upset and most unpleasant company. One morning she seemed even more troubled than usual. She told me that Elaine had run away. She was gone without a trace. It had been a foolish thing to do. How could she survive all alone in the forest? She would be attacked by wild animals or die of the cold.

The news delighted me. Now no one would ever know that I was Gloria. I told Mother this, and that it was stupid to be concerned about Elaine. She meant only trouble for us. We should be glad she was gone.

That was the day Prince John returned to Castle

Idris. But I never spoke to him. I saw him ride into the
castle when I went to the window to see what all the
clatter was about. This time he was accompanied by
only a squire and a handful of bowmen. Perhaps I was
imagining it, but an urgency seemed to drive the party
and especially Prince John. No sooner had he entered
the hall, it seemed, than he left it, jumped on his horse,
and rode off again.

After that I lay down to rest in order to look my best
that evening. But the prince did not come to supper.
Mother was mystified. She had entertained him in her
chamber shortly before the meal. He had been in excellent health and spirits, she said.

After supper Mother went to the prince's chamber to
be sure that he was all right. He was not there. Then
she and some of her ladies looked everywhere for him.
They did not find him. His horse stood in the stables.
John had not walked out of the gate—the porter in the
lodge had not seen him since he had returned to the
castle an hour before supper. Mother then instituted a
complete search of the castle. Prince John was not
found.

When he did not appear the following morning,
Mother sent every man she could spare out into the
hills and forest to search for the prince. His squire and
bowmen joined the search party, but John was not
found. He seemed to have disappeared.

That afternoon Mother decided to look for Prince
John herself. It was absurd for her to do this, and I
told her so. If all the men at the castle could not find
the prince, she could not hope to. But she said that it
would look well and would show everyone how concerned she was. And she advised me to accompany
her. I refused. Above all else I hated riding a mule. But
Mother finally convinced me that it was necessary for
appearance's sake, so I agreed to go with her.

We rode to the village and asked several women
there if they had seen the prince. They had seen him
ride through the village toward the castle with his
party, but had not seen him since.

After that we rode beyond the village and began to circle back through the forest to the castle. Soon we found ourselves on a track which Mother did not remember. It led into a deep valley of tall trees. The light was dim there. It was an eerie place. I did not like it, and began to fear that we were lost.

I had become quite certain of this when we saw ahead of us a man of whom we could ask directions. He stood before the mouth of a cave which resembled a huge jar turned on its side. The man was evidently a hermit. He held a lighted lantern above his head as if to illumine anyone who passed before him. And as we drew nearer, I saw that he held something against his breast.

It was a small chest of unusual design and beauty. Its lid stood open, displaying a mass of precious gems of every size and color. We reined our mounts to a halt before the hermit. Both Mother and I were speechless at the sight of such riches.

Before we could say anything, the hermit asked me who I was. I did not like his tone and told him that it was none of his business, but that I was the daughter of the Duke of Idris. Then I asked him how such a low-born person came to possess such jewels when I had none at all.

The hermit told me that the stones did not belong to him, but were the treasure of a great queen who anxiously awaited their return. The hermit had traveled a long distance to give the jewels back to their rightful owner, but now he could walk no further. He asked me then if I would carry the treasure to the queen for him. Since I was the daughter of a noble lord, he knew he could trust me to do this. Would I not carry the treasure to its owner, who waited only a short distance up the road?

I agreed to do so, telling the hermit that he could trust his very life to me if necessary. So he closed the lid of the box, gave it to me, described the queen so that I would recognize her, and thanked me profusely for helping him.

Mother and I rode on. The chest was heavy and I clutched it tightly to me. We turned off the road as soon as we could and found our way back to Castle Idris. We had no intention of giving the jewels to anyone. Mother and I decided to keep them for ourselves. We had not even needed to discuss the matter.

After we had returned safely to the castle, Mother told me that the jewels would be my dowry. And that if Prince John had somehow perished, I would marry his younger brother, Prince William, instead.

I found this agreeable, certainly, but one thing about the day's adventure annoyed me: I could not open the chest. It seemed to be locked. I wished to examine and admire the jewels it contained, and declared that we must get the smith to force it open for us. But Mother said that would ruin the box. It was such a beautiful one, and if it was spoiled, we would have nothing as fine in which to present the jewels to the king. And since we did not want anyone to know we possessed such a treasure, it would be better to leave the chest alone and hide it until it was time to carry it to Tintagal.

That was also the day we discovered what had happened to Prince John.

Chapter Fourteen

****

Elaine's Story

It was an animal that had appeared on the hilltop. It stood still, looking down at me for a moment. Then it raised its head and howled at the sky—a short, whining howl that rose in volume to a triumphant pitch.

It was a wolf. It rushed at me. Its black shape flew down the shadowed slope like a great wingless bird skimming the ground on a swift current of wind.

I screamed and ran from it. But I had no sooner moved, it seemed, than the beast was at my heels. I glanced back at it, tripped, and sprawled to the ground.

The wolf pounced upon me and straddled me. It was about to snap at my throat, I thought, when a second howl pierced the night. The wolf froze, staring at the hilltop above us. I followed his gaze. Three more wolves stood silhouetted against the dim sky.

As we watched, all three raised their heads and howled an eerie harmonic challenge. Then they ran toward us, halting thirty feet away. They were gray

wolves. Two remained still, but the third, the largest
of the three, advanced slowly toward us, his ears
thrust forward, his tail stretched straight out behind
him, his teeth bared.

The black wolf left me, and in the same posture,
growling viciously, he stalked the gray challenger. The
two beasts crept toward each other until they were
only a few feet apart. Then each halted, appraising
its adversary.

During those hushed moments I wondered if it
would be more painful to be torn to pieces slowly by
one wolf or more quickly by three. Clearly neither the
black wolf nor the gray ones had any intention of
sharing their supper with the other.

Suddenly the two wolves lunged at each other and
met in a snarling, thrashing, twisted mass of fur and
snapping jaws.

My only thought was of escape. I scrambled to my
feet and ran as fast as I could, leaving the battle further and further behind me. The gray wolf's companions did not pursue me: they remained, I saw in a
backward glance, motionless, watching the conflict.

I could hear the sounds of it behind me as I ran,
and I hoped it would continue long enough for me to
get away. But all too soon it was over. Looking back,
I saw the three gray wolves slink away. The lead one
limped, his head hung low, his tail dragged the grass.

The black wolf leaped after me, and in an instant
he was upon me. I was too terrified to run or scream.
I stood, tense, my hand clutching my throat, waiting
for that final leap and the pain of his teeth tearing at
my flesh.

I remember nothing more until I felt something wet
on my cheek, upon my eyelids. Something was licking
my face. I turned my head aside. The licking continued. I tried to push whatever it was away. My hand
brushed huge, dripping teeth and a furry snout. I
opened my eyes, knowing then that I felt the wolf's
face.

I sat up, pushing the animal away.

"No!" I cried. "No! No! No!"

The wolf did not molest me further. He sat before me on his haunches for perhaps half a minute, beating the ground with his tail. We stared at each other. I could think only of the glare of battle I had seen in the wolf's eyes before he had leaped at the gray wolf.

"No!" I cried again.

In reply the wolf whined almost pitifully and rolled upon his back. His legs pointed to the sky; his paws drooped. He turned his head and gazed at me, his tail thrashing the ground.

I was too astonished to move or make a sound. The animal turned over and groveled slowly—inch by inch —to me, his tail wagging all the while. Then he licked my hand.

Still I did not move.

When he had finished, he simply lay there quietly, gazing at my face. I could not be sure because it was quite dark by then, but I thought he smiled. Slowly I lifted my hand and touched the back of his neck. He laid his chin on my stomach, and I stroked his head.

"Do you want to be a friend?" I asked.

The wolf's tail pounded the ground faster and faster, and he lifted his head and whined.

"Do you want to be my friend?" I asked again. "Can you understand me?"

At this the wolf leaped to his feet and pranced and romped back and forth before me. Then he returned, crouched beside me, and nuzzled my arm.

"Then I shall have to give you a name," I said. I tried to hold my voice steady. "I shall call you Wolf." I hoped desperately that Wolf's behavior was not an animal's trick of some kind.

Wolf whined, but I could not tell whether in objection or consent.

I looked up at the dark sky. A snowflake landed on my cheek.

"But we cannot stay here, Wolf. Not out in the open like this. What shall we do?"

I did not really believe that the animal could understand what I said, but talking to him calmed me and made me feel brave. "We should find a cave or shelter of some kind. But how can we do that in the dark?"

Wolf leaped to his feet then and ran off. Had I frightened him away? Had it all been a game with him? Was I to be left all alone after all? In the dark?

I began to walk toward a peak which I could see dimly outlined against the sky, but almost at once I struck my foot on a rock and nearly fell. I could never walk in that darkness. I knew it was useless to try. I was able to see a huge angular shape off to my left. It was a boulder, and I sat down against it and pulled my cloak about me.

As I did so, I thought of what Brian had told me about Mortmoor—about the quicksand and the mists and how no one lost there at night would live to see the morning. I shuddered. *I* was lost on Mortmoor.

Sir Tor had had his revenge. Only he could have been so barbarous as to lead me into this wilderness and abandon me here. He could not kill me quickly. No, I must suffer before I died. How much would I suffer when the gray wolves returned or before I perished from the cold?

Chapter Fifteen

✣✣✣✣✣✣✣✣✣✣✣✣✣✣✣✣✣✣✣✣

Elaine's Story

My thoughts were interrupted by the rustle of grass, a whine, and then a cold nose on my neck. Wolf had returned. He grasped my cloak in his mouth and pulled. When I stood, he began to walk away, pulling me with him.

I grasped the long fur at his shoulders. He seemed to understand that he could lead me that way, and let go of my cloak. Wolf led me to a sheltered place. It did not quite apear to be a cave, but there seemed to be a rock roof of sorts. And the ground was covered with a thick layer of dry grass which, I supposed, the wind had blown there.

I lay down, pulling my cloak tightly about me. And Wolf lay down beside me.

I lived to see the morning. I had slept fitfully, dreaming horrible dreams. In my sleep I had huddled close to Wolf; even so, I had not been warm. But I had lived to see the morning on Mortmoor. And as I

sat gazing out of the covert, I was exultant about it.
Now that I had lived through one night, I would live
through as many nights as it might take to cross the
wilderness and reach habitation.

. But it did not look as though I would walk far that
day. The snow had turned to rain during the night.
The rain, bringing warmer weather, had departed
now, leaving behind a bright mist that screened the
moor from view.

Wolf lay asleep by my side. I had not seen him in
daylight. I looked down at him, admiring his thick
raven-black coat. He stirred, sat up groggily, gazed
about, stood, stretched, shook himself, and then sat
down beside me.

He looked up at me then, and I gasped. I gazed
back into a pair of startlingly brilliant blue eyes. Was
it possible? No! No, I was imagining things. Why
should not a wolf have blue eyes? It must have been
Wolf's black fur that made them seem so intensely
blue. The color of— No, I would not even think it.

Nevertheless I stroked Wolf's head and murmured,
"What have they done to you?"

Wolf did not reply; instead he nuzzled my arm.
Then he turned away, stood, and ran out into the
mist. I felt certain he would return, and he did—almost five minutes later. Again he grasped my cloak
in his mouth as if to pull me to my feet.

"We cannot go out in this, Wolf," I said, gesturing
to the mist. "It is too wet and we could not be able to
see our way."

But Wolf paid no attention to me. He continued to
tug at my cloak. So I stood and, against my better
judgment, followed him outside. He led me down a
gentle grassy hillside to a group of bramble bushes.
At their base a spring bubbled out of the ground.
Wolf drank from the stream it made, leaving the
sparkling pool to me. I drank deeply, and then, my
thirst assuaged, I splashed the icy water on my face.

"Were you as thirsty as I?" I asked Wolf. He

wagged his tail rapidly. "You were? If only you could do as well with breakfast." Wolf's ears pricked. "No, no raw rabbit or mouse for me, please. At least—not yet."

Now it became brighter, and my shadow slowly appeared on the ground before me. The sun shone through the mist and a breeze brushed my cheek. The weather would clear.

Wolf stood beside me, looking quietly about.

"What shall we do, Wolf?" I asked.

He looked up at me.

"Where shall we go? Not back to Castle Idris—not back to Sir Tor. We may be lost, but at least I am free of him. Could we find the road, do you think? Then we could go to Tintagal." I looked down into Wolf's blue eyes, studying them for a moment. "I know Prince John. He would help us, or his father would, surely."

Wolf pranced and romped before me and wagged his tail.

"Could you take me there? Could we go west? Do you know which way that is?"

Wolf whined and darted off in the opposite direction from the stream. He stopped running twenty feet or so up the slope, looked back at me, wagged his tail, and waited.

So Wolf led and I followed him across the moor. Seldom did we descend to the valleys between the hills where mires and bogs might be and where reeds grew. We went around them. The fresh breeze had cleared the mist almost before we had left the spring. All day the sky lay blue behind a dome of great lavender and cream-colored clouds. Their shadows skimmed the hills before us, urging us onward. On such a day, in spite of being hungry and tired of walking, it was good to be alive.

By late afternoon the landscape had changed a little. Now the hills rose more precipitously and were divided by coombs. In these steep valleys dwarf oak, hawthorn, holly, and gorse grew. And mountain ashes and willows bore old ravens' nests. We saw rabbits and, far down in one coomb, a deer.

We found a track which must have borne west because Wolf led me down it. Soon, as we descended into a coomb, I was astonished to see sheep grazing. And there beside the path below us their shepherd lay on a sheepskin.

Propped on his elbows, he gazed dreamily into the distance. He did not see or hear us until we were almost upon him. Then he jumped to his feet, staring at us, grabbed his bow from the ground and an arrow from the quiver that had lain beside it. He strung the arrow to his bow and raised it, but before he could take aim, I jumped in front of Wolf.

"Would you shoot a helpless woman, shepherd?" I cried. "Put down your bow. We mean you no harm."

The shepherd hesitated, undecided what to do. But he did not lower his bow.

"I am the Lady Elaine, daughter of the Duke of Idris," I said more quickly. "If you kill me, you will answer to him."

"The Duke of Idris is dead," the shepherd said.

He lowered his bow, but he kept the arrow ready.

"My father is not dead. I spoke to him not a fortnight ago."

"He's been dead for ten years."

I walked to the shepherd then, and Wolf followed close behind me.

"I thought that was a dog," the shepherd growled, "but it is a wolf. I know a wolf when I see one."

As he spoke, he glanced at the hillside above us. The shepherd's dog silently cowered there, staring at Wolf.

"He is my friend," I said. "He will not harm you or your sheep. Put aside your bow."

The shepherd did not put it aside, nor did he reply. Instead he glared menacingly at Wolf and then at me. He was a short, sinewy old man with a wrinkled, ruddy face and tiny glinting eyes.

"If you shoot me, shepherd, Wolf will be at your throat before you can seize another arrow. And if you shoot him . . ."

At that moment a shadow swept across the shepherd. A raven had flown between him and the sun. The great blackbird looked down at us as it circled not far above our heads. Then it flew off.

"Death bird," the shepherd murmured with a shudder as he watched the raven fly away.

"And if you shoot Wolf," I repeated, "you will have me to deal with."

"You?" the shepherd replied. He recoiled from me, wide-eyed. His hands trembled. "What do you want?"

"Only some food and the way to Tintagal."

"Begone! My food is mine."

"But we have not eaten for days."

"That is none of my doing."

"Would you send us on without giving us something to eat?"

The shepherd glared at me. He was hostile; yet at the same time he seemed frightened.

"You must help us," I said. When he did not speak, I added, "As you would wish to be helped."

"I need no help." He pointed down the path. "Now go!"

"You might need help. Suppose something happened to you or your sheep. You are all alone out here. Would you not ask for help then?"

"What are you going to do?" His eyes grew wide. His bow and arrow slipped from his hands to the ground.

He turned from me and ran up the hillside to a leather sack which lay on the ground. He opened it and drew out a piece of meat and an orange cheese. He broke the cheese in two, casting half of it back into the sack. Then he dashed to me and tossed the meat and cheese into my arms. But he did not touch me. He drew back, trembling as if in alarm or horror.

"Thank you," I said. "And I have been so cold. Would you give me one of your sheepskins?"

"Take it." The man pointed to the sheepskin he had been lying on.

I draped it over my arm and cradled the meat and cheese in its folds.

"And can you tell me the way to Tintagal? Is there a road nearby?"

The man pointed down the path. "The road is that way. Now go! For God's sake, go!" the shepherd shouted. "And don't come back. And don't send any of your kind. Leave me and my sheep alone!" He crossed himself again and again.

I thought the man had gone mad.

"Thank you," I said, and walked hurriedly down the path away from him. Wolf walked ahead of me, and soon we rounded a hillside, out of the shepherd's sight.

A hundred yards farther on I sat down to eat beside a mountain stream. I could not wait another moment. I was ravenous and so was Wolf. He did not care for cheese, so I gave him dried meat.

As I ate, I thought about the shepherd. He had certainly been unfriendly. But it was not his antagonism that puzzled me, it was his fright. He had seemed to be terrified of me and at the same time horrified. I knew that the shadow of a raven meant death, but that had nothing to do with me. He had thought I had planned to do something to him. What? Had he thought I would harm him in some way? And what had he meant by "your kind?" He had said, "And don't send any of your kind."

"What did he mean by 'your kind'?" I asked Wolf. Wolf looked at me wisely, as though he knew.

"If only you could talk. Well, we must go on." I stood. "It will soon be dark, and we must find a place to spend the night. It is going to be cold, I think."

We drank from the stream and then proceeded down the path. It led to a road, which we soon discovered winding along below us. A wild moorland pony peeked out at us from behind a rocky outcropping. Then it bolted away, terrified, I suppose, that Wolf would pursue it. I glanced quickly at Wolf. He stood tense, gazing after the pony as if wanting to chase it. But he did not leave me.

We spent the night there, partly sheltered by the rocks. The next morning Wolf caught a stoat for breakfast. I ate some of the cheese. The rest of the food I would carry with me. But I dreaded the prospect of carrying the sheepskin over my arm all day as I walked. It had kept me warm during the night, and I knew I would need it on other nights. So I spent a half-hour making a long vest of it simply by cutting two slits with my knife for armholes. Tied about the waist with a thong cut from the same skin, I would wear the vest under my cloak.

When I had finished, we set out again—down the path to the road. When we reached it, Wolf turned without hesitation to the right, and we walked that way.

Day after day the moor stretched before us: even from the high hills we could see no end to it. How lonely and bleak it was, without a soul to meet along the way. But as we traveled, I often felt that someone was near, that I was being watched. I had begun to sense this after we had struck the road, and the feeling would not leave me. I found myself looking about, but I never saw anyone.

Without abating, my feeling persisted. We had begun to descend from the highlands now, and though the land remained rocky, oaks and clumps of pines grew beside the road. Sparrow hawks and kestrels circled above us.

It was as I looked up at them that I noticed a man on horseback behind us. He rode along the brow of a hill where we had walked ten minutes before.

"See, Wolf?" I said, pointing to the rider. "We are about to have company. Perhaps he can tell us where we are and if there is a village or dwelling of any kind nearby."

We paused to watch the horseman. He vanished for a moment as the road dipped out of sight. Then he galloped into view again. As he drew nearer, I could see that he was a squat man. And I sensed something familiar in his posture.

"Wolf!" I cried. "Come quickly!"

Chapter Sixteen

✽✦✽✦✽✦✽✦✽✦✽✦✽✦✽✦✽✦✽✦✽

Elaine's Story

I dashed from the road into a coppice of oak and pine. There a tall, square block of granite thrust itself out of the earth. Wolf and I hid behind the rock and peered out between the tree branches to watch the horseman pass. As he drew near I prayed that he had not seen us from the hilltop.

Presently Sir Tor thundered past. He galloped at full tilt, urging his sweating horse to even greater speed. He hunched forward in the saddle, glaring straight ahead. Though his lips were parted, he clenched his teeth. And as he rode by, one hand felt the hilt of his sword.

He had gone. He had not seen us.

I waited until I could barely hear the sound of his horse. Then I said to Wolf, "It was Sir Tor. He came to kill me."

Wolf looked up at me almost as though in disbelief.

"But how did he know where I was?" I asked. "He knew! It was no coincidence that he rode down this very road at this very time."

I mused, then said, "He will return when he does not find me. We cannot go by road any longer. We must go through the forest. Take me westward, Wolf. Lead me through the woods to Tintagal."

We spent the night in the hollow trunk of an enormous fallen beech, and then walked on. We passed through a deep forest of oak. Though it was winter, the great trees clung to their brown leaves; so despite the blue sky above, the light beneath them was dim. The spongy ground lay umber-colored under the trees, flecked with cinnamon by beams of dancing sunlight.

During the afternoon the forest grew denser still, and I was glad when Wolf found a path and led me down it. A few minutes later we came upon a man standing before the mouth of a cave. I was not only surprised to find another human being in that place, I was surprised to see a cave as well, since the forest had been almost level for miles. The cave's smooth, rocky dome resembled nothing so much as a huge jar resting on its side and sunk partly into the earth.

The man who stood before it—a hermit, I supposed—was a robust, middle-aged man of medium height with chestnut hair and beard. He wore an undyed woolen robe draped around his waist and over his shoulder in an unfamiliar manner. Since he was alone, I was not afraid to approach him.

Three things puzzled me about the hermit: He held a lighted lantern above his head as though it would help him see anyone who passed by. The daylight was dim, I thought, but the afternoon had not grown dark enough for that. Then, his expression as he gazed at me was one of unmitigated skepticism. Why, I wondered, should he be doubtful or suspicious of me? We had never met before. And third and most perplexing of all, he held a small chest of dull-colored metal against his breast. The box was worked in a lovely pattern of flowers and birds in low relief. Its lid hung open, displaying a mass of jewels. The gems were of different sizes, and flashed with many-colored fire. I was fascinated by their radiance. Were they merely stones or were they blazing stars?

But then I realized how dangerous it was to display such splendor in that manner. Suppose I were a robber? I looked up at the hermit, troubled and speechless.

"What is your name, maiden?" he asked.

"I am the Lady Elaine," I replied. "My father is the Duke of Idris. We are traveling to Tintagal. Will this path take us in the right direction? Is there a road nearby which will lead us there?"

"Ah, you are going to Tintagal," he said. "Yes, the path leads in that direction, and you can do me a great kindness along the way."

"Oh? What is that, reverend hermit?"

The hermit set his lantern on the ground and snapped the lid of the chest shut. Offering it to me, he said, "Will you take this chest to a lady who waits for it a mile farther along the path?"

"Take the chest?" I asked incredulously. "But why? No! No, I could not do that."

"Why could you not do that? It is not so heavy that you could not carry it. You are going in that direction. You will pass by her. Why can you not carry it to her?"

"Because it is of great value. And you do not know me. How could you trust me with such a thing? I might run off with it and keep it for myself."

"But you are the daughter of a noble lord," the hermit said. "You would not do that."

"Can you not carry it there yourself?" I asked.

"I have carried it a long way—across lands and seas—but I can walk no farther. My feet will not carry me another step."

"Then rest awhile, good hermit, and go on later."

"Alas, then I would arrive too late. She waits for me within the hour. She is Queen Hecuba and these are her jewels. She will die of disappointment if I do not return them to her. And if I do not arrive at the appointed time, she will think them lost."

"Surely she would wait."

"No, she will believe that I have perished and that her jewels are lost."

"How far have you traveled, reverend hermit?"

"Through many lands."

"And you can walk no farther? But you look so well."

The hermit sat down on a rock then and sighed. "No, I am too tired. I cannot walk another step."

I looked at Wolf, who had been quietly studying the hermit. He looked back at me questioningly.

"But suppose I met robbers? I would never forgive myself for losing the gems."

The hermit stood, carried the chest to the rear of the cave, and returned carrying a basket and a piece of cloth. I noticed that he walked without difficulty. He placed the chest in the basket and covered it with the cloth. Then he handed the basket to me by the handle.

"Take it, Lady," he said. "No one will know what you carry. Must we not help each other? Will you not oblige a tired old man, and save Her Grace from grief and despair? She waits just up the path. You need not go out of your way. You will pass before her."

I took the basket then and said, "How will I know her? Where will she be?"

The hermit's thin lips smiled. Then he said, "About a mile from here the path will cross a meadow. In the center of the meadow stands a mighty oak. You will find Queen Hecuba standing beneath it. She will be dressed in brown silk and she will wear a gold crown."

"How do you know what she will wear?" I asked.

"She always wears the same," the hermit replied.

I had examined the cave as we had talked, and so had Wolf. I had seen him sniffing about in it. It was empty and seemed uninhabited. I saw no bed or pallet nor anything that might contain food. So I did not ask the hermit for anything to eat. I merely said that

I would take the basket to Queen Hecuba. Then I wished him good day, and Wolf and I left him.

The chest proved heavier than I had thought, and every few minutes I shifted the basket from one hand to the other. I wondered if Queen Hecuba would be waiting for me and what I would do if she was not.

I need not have been concerned about that. When I reached the meadow, I saw the massive oak tree just as the hermit had described it. Beneath it a woman paced back and forth. She was tall with an ample figure and a large bosom, which she carried regally. She may have been sixty years old or more, and she wore a gold crown in her gray hair.

"Well, so you have come at last," she called as I approached her. "You are late."

"We came as quickly as we could," I said.

The woman looked down at Wolf disapprovingly. Then she said, "I am not used to being kept waiting. One would think, after coming all this distance to stand out in the cold in this barren field, that at least things would go according to schedule. One might expect it, I suppose. He was never very thoughtful—always thinking about that ridiculous quest. Well?" She extended her hand to me. "Give it to me!"

"You are Queen Hecuba?" I said.

"I am Queen Harmonia."

"But the hermit said I was to give the basket to Queen Hecuba."

"Yes, yes, of course. Harmonia, Hecuba—what does it matter?"

"It could matter a great deal. I must be certain to give it to the right person."

"Did he tell you that I would be waiting here in this frozen field under this tree, that I would be dressed in brown silk, that I would be wearing my gold crown? Did he tell you that the chest of jewels which you carry in that basket belongs to me and that he was bringing it to me, but that he could walk no farther?"

"Yes, but—"

"Well, then, use your intelligence, child. How could I be anyone but the right person? They are my jewels. Give them to me."

I handed her the basket. She lifted the chest out of it, and then returned the basket to me.

"Thank you, but I shan't need the basket," I said. "It might be better if you carried the chest in it. It looks terribly conspicuous, carrying it that way."

"My dear child, you may find that you *do* need the basket, and I suggest you take it with you. And"—she drew something from the décolletage of her gown—"here is something for you. It is a token of my gratitude."

She handed me a tiny blue glass bottle stopped with a cork.

"Thank you," I said. I held it up to the light. "What a pretty color. What is it?"

"A bottle," the queen said disdainfully. "But never mind what it is. It is what it contains that matters."

"What does it contain?"

"My tears. Tears that I have shed at the loss of my precious jewels." She screwed up her features in an expression of anguish for a moment. "Guard them well. They shall be part of your dowry."

"My dowry?"

"Your dowry."

I gazed at her, bewildered.

"It is important that your dowry be more splendid than your rival's."

"But I don't have a rival, and I don't need a dowry because I don't plan to marry. And if I did, I cannot imagine how tears could be considered very splendid. Of course, I am delighted to have them."

"I have no time for silly observations. If you are intelligent, you will do as I say. Now, go along. I am very busy. I have many things to do."

"But, Your Grace, I cannot leave you here all alone like this. It is cold and you have no cloak. Where will you go? What will you do?"

The queen closed her eyes for several moments.

Then she opened them, looked down at me, and said, "I am perfectly capable of taking care of myself. Now, please go along like a good girl, and take that horrible animal with you."

I thanked her again and then I left her. I did not care for Queen Hecuba or Harmonia or whatever her name was at all. I did not like her calling Wolf a horrible animal, and I thought she was rude. Wolf and I walked away from her without looking back, and soon after we entered the wood again, I decided to discard the basket. There was no point, certainly, in carrying along an empty basket which I would have no use for, especially since it seemed to be getting heavier.

But first I looked inside it. There beneath the cloth lay a loaf of bread, dried meat, cheese, hard-cooked eggs, and a bottle of wine.

Wolf caught rabbits and mice, leaving the food in the basket entirely to me. He was fortunate: a plentiful supply of food for him roamed the woods, but I had to make the meat, bread, cheese, and eggs that had materialized in the bottom of the basket last as long as possible. Several days later the basket stood empty, and I threw it away.

We had been favored with good weather and had had little difficulty in finding sheltered places to spend the nights. But then one morning, heavy dark-gray clouds crowded into the sky. They hung so low that it seemed one could almost touch them. During the afternoon they began to drop their burden of sleet and wet snow upon us.

We would have welcomed the dense forest then, but we had left it behind, having found a neglected road which seemed to lead westward. The road wound across gently rolling land which looked as though it might have been farmed once. Now it lay choked with coppices of oak saplings, alders, hazels, and sycamores —all young trees which could provide no protection against the weather. Nor was there any kind of structure visible anywhere to offer us shelter.

So we continued walking. Soon my cloak became damp, Wolf's fur carried a thin crust of sugary-looking ice, and the road turned to muddy puddles.

Then, nearly at dusk, after I had resigned myself to walking all night, we saw a person sitting beside the road on a ruined wall.

Chapter Seventeen

✵✵✵✵✵✵✵✵✵✵✵✵✵✵✵✵✵✵✵✵

Elaine's Story

It was an old woman, I discovered as we drew near her. She sat swathed in a heavy cloak, her face almost hidden by its generous hood. In the shadows beneath it, I could barely see the terribly wrinkled skin around her nose and mouth.

"Why are you out on a night like this, dearie?" she asked. "Where are you going in all this wet? And what a pretty doggie."

Wolf growled. His hackles rose.

"Wolf!" I said. "Be quiet, please."

"Nice doggie," the woman said.

"We are going to Tintagal," I said. "Is there a house or cottage nearby where we can spend the night?"

"Oh, yes, dearie. There surely is. You can spend the night with me if you like."

"We would be ever so grateful, good dame, if we could. I am damp and nearly chilled through."

"Of course, dearie. You will stay at my castle tonight with me. Tomorrow will be clear, and you can go on your way then."

"Your castle?" I asked.

"You will see it on the hill there." She pointed up the road. "Walk to the break in the wall and up the track, and you will see it. Run along."

"But aren't you coming?"

"Go along, dearie, and I will come as soon as I can."

"Can't you come with us now?"

"I—I will wait here until a gentleman passes. He will have a letter for me, and I want it."

"Then we will wait and keep you company."

"No, no. You will catch your death. Why, you are damp and chilled to the bone. That is plain to see. Go and get in out of the wet, child. You will find the castle easily enough. Do as I say. I will be there directly."

The old hag seemed terribly insistent that I go on ahead of her, so, not wanting to displease her, I obliged.

The track wound up a slope through rank grass and thickets of scrub. Once it had been a cart track: its two ruts were plainly visible in the long grass. But now oak and ash saplings thrust from the earth like long needles, and bracken lay withered between the furrows. No cart had traveled this path for a long time, and I wondered how such a ruined way could lead to the meanest hovel, let alone a castle.

But it did lead to a castle. We saw it shortly, veiled in mist, on top of the rise before us. It was not very impressive: merely three square stone towers of different heights huddled together and shrouded with black-green ivy. It had no moat, but a wall surrounded its yard and formed one side of a barn. The yard was clogged with brambles and brush. Not even a path led to the wooden stair which climbed the outside of the building to, I supposed, the door to the hall.

The stairway was rotten and dangerous, and the

door stood ajar. When we reached it, we found the old hag sitting just inside, waiting for us.

She cackled and said, "I thought you would never come, dearie. Been admiring the view?"

"How did you get here so fast?" I asked.

"I know a path, but you would never have found it. Oh, no!" She pointed at Wolf. "We don't allow doggies in here. He will have to stay outside."

"Then I am afraid I cannot accept your hospitality, good dame," I said. "I could not leave him out in this weather. But thank you nevertheless for your kindness."

"Now, now, dearie. I did not mean he would have to stay out in the wet. Of course not! It is not a fit night for man nor beast. He can sleep in the barn and be dry and comfy in the hay there. Just as dry and comfy as you will be in a bed of your own."

I glanced at Wolf. He looked up at me, and then he growled at the poor woman, his ears pricked forward, his tail held horizontally. Then without warning he leaped past us into the hall. It was a large room, and it took a few moments for Wolf to circle it. Then he dashed to the stairway and up it.

I could only stand gaping, amazed. But when Wolf disappeared from view, I ran after him.

The old woman called after me: "He can't stay in here. You must take him out! You must . . . "

But I heard no more because of the clatter of my footsteps on the stone stairs. By the time I had found Wolf, he had already investigated two of the chambers there. I followed him into the remaining one. But I had no sooner entered the room than Wolf bounded past me and out of it. Now he flew up the stairway to the top floor. I imagine he had seen the two rooms there by the time I had climbed the stairs because he waited for me on the landing, sitting quietly on his haunches and looking at me rather defiantly, I thought.

I went to him and squatted in front of him. "What is it, Wolf? What is the matter?"

Wolf growled, but he did not growl at me—he looked toward the stairs.

"Is he up there?" the hag called, apparently from the second-floor landing.

"Yes," I called back. "I will bring him down." Then I said, "Come, Wolf." I grasped his fur at the shoulders. "We have to go outside. You cannot stay here."

Wolf growled again. But this time he growled at me, and I let go of him.

"Come along," I said.

I descended the stairs and Wolf followed me.

"I will take him out to the barn," I said to the woman as I passed her on the landing. "I am terribly sorry."

Wolf followed me down to the hall, out the door, and down the wooden stairway to the ground. But as I turned toward the barn, he grasped my cloak in his mouth and began to pull me toward the track which led to the road. I grasped my cloak and snatched it away from him. Again he grabbed it, but this time I could not wrench it from his mouth no matter how hard I tugged at it.

"Wolf!" I cried. "Stop it! What are you trying to do? Let go! Let *go!*"

The fabric tore as I tried once again to pull my cloak away from him. Furious, I slapped his face with the palm of my hand. He released me then, drawing back in astonishment.

"I have tramped all day in the cold and drizzle," I cried at Wolf. "I am tired. Tired! And cold and hungry. And I want to sleep in a *bed*. I am tired of sleeping on the ground. And I am tired of your—your stupid, unreasonable behavior. You will sleep in the barn, and I will sleep in a bed in a chamber in a *civilized* manner."

With that I stomped off toward the barn. I would show Wolf where to sleep. If he followed me there, all well and good. If not, he could go off and good riddance.

He did follow me there. The barn was dry inside, and a pile of old hay lay heaped in the corner.

"Sleep here!" I said, hardly glancing at Wolf. "I will come back in the morning."

I marched out of the building, leaving the barn door ajar in the event Wolf wanted to go hunting for his supper. Then I returned to the castle, where the old woman waited for me. She had descended to the hall and now sat in her chair just inside the doorway.

I said, "I am terribly sorry, Dame . . . "

"Winet," the old woman said.

"And I am Elaine. My father is the Duke of Idris. I am so terribly sorry, Dame Winet. I do not know what was the matter with him."

"Oh, that's all right, dearie. Doggies will be doggies. Now, you run along up. Take the chamber to your right at the top of the stairs. You must be exhausted from all the cold and all that walking. There's a nice big bed waiting for you."

"But—but aren't you going to have supper? Aren't you going to take off your cloak? It must be wet! Aren't—aren't you cold? There is no fire. Won't you light a fire?"

The woman threw back her hood then, releasing a thick, tangled nest of long hair which fell about her face and neck, hiding even more of her features than the hood had. Perhaps if it had been lighter I would have been able to see her better, but it was almost dark by then and it was difficult to see anything but the dimmest shapes in the dusk.

"I would, dearie," she said. "But there's nothing to build one with."

"There must be wood. There are trees growing all about the castle."

"Yes, but I don't have anybody to cut them for me, dearie."

"No one to cut them? But you must have someone. Isn't there someone to do the work? Cook? Take care of the animals—the house?"

"Oh, no, dearie, not for a long time."

"You are all alone here?"

"Oh, yes. All alone."

"How do you manage? Who cooks your food? Who—"

"It doesn't take much food when you get as old as I. One lives on practically nothing then—hardly a mouthful." She cackled. "It doesn't take much to keep an old crone like me alive, no indeed."

"But you must eat *something*."

"Once in a while somebody brings me something."

"You—you have nothing here?"

"To eat? Oh, no, dearie. I wish I could give you a proper supper, but that would cost money and I haven't any. Not since my poor old husband died and left me all alone, you see."

"I am so sorry," I said. If there was to be no fire or supper, I thought, I might as well go to bed. "Well— I shall go on up then. Is there a candle or—"

"A candle?" She laughed again. "Where would I get a candle? They cost money and I haven't got any. But you can find your way. There's the stairs. Open your eyes wide and you will see them. Now, go along and have a nice sleep."

I left her then. Opening my eyes as wide as I could, I did discern the stairs. It was totally dark now—black inside the stairwell. But when I had felt my way up it and had reached the second-floor landing, enough light shone through a window to outline the doorway of my room.

Inside, I felt for the bed, shivering with the damp cold of those stone walls and breaking through sticky veiled cobwebs, which clung to my face and hands. Finally I found the bed, climbed into it without removing my cloak, and pulled the covers about me in a cloud of dust.

The dust made me cough, and the mattress was uncomfortable: it sagged terribly and was lumpy. The woolen sheets, now a vast web of holes, pulled apart at the touch.

I was so tired that I had expected to fall asleep at

once regardless of the condition of the bed, but I did not. I lay awake thinking of Wolf. I wished I had not struck him. Why had I been so cruel?

Then a thought occurred to me that tugged at my heart: suppose Wolf should go away now and leave me? Suppose he had come to hate me for striking him? Somehow I had felt that he was more than just an animal. Was he? No, only an animal would have behaved as capriciously as Wolf had when we arrived at the castle. I had misled myself in order to keep from being lonely. And what would I do now that we were entering civilized country? How could I manage Wolf if he continued to act as he had tonight?

I must have drifted off to sleep then or perhaps I had merely closed my eyes. But suddenly with a start I was wide awake. I had heard a sound—a footstep. And I thought I heard breathing. I turned my head and stared at the doorway. Was someone standing there?

I listened, but I heard no sound. And it was too dark to see. Suddenly footsteps pounded the floor, and a figure dashed past the window toward me. Something flashed, reflecting light. And then a deafening cry—half howl, half growl—rent the air. A heavy object crashed to the floor beside my bed, and a vicious snarl was drowned in a scream of pain. Then the room was still.

During the tumult I had sat up. Now I tried desperately to see what lay beside my bed. Something leaped at me. I screamed, pushing it away with the palms of my hands.

But then I felt a wet tongue licking my fingers. Wolf stood on the bed. He licked my face. I threw my arms around his ice-cold body and clasped him tightly to me.

"Wolf!" I cried. "Oh, Wolf! What have you done?"

Chapter Eighteen

✱✱✱✱✱✱✱✱✱✱✱✱✱✱✱✱✱✱✱✱

Elaine's Story

I held onto Wolf tightly, staring at the still, dark shape on the floor. Then I slipped out of the bed, and squatted beside it. Wolf jumped down beside me, whining.

A figure lay there. I touched it. It seemed to be a man. Yes, it was a man—flat chest, thick arms, bearded jaw. Oh, God! The man's throat had a hole in it. Around the hole a soft, slippery mass of pulp was wet. His neck was wet. The floor was wet. The man was dead.

"Who is it, Wolf?" I asked. "Where is Dame Winet?" I rose to my feet. "Come, we must find her."

"Dame Winet?" I called when we reached the landing. "Dame Winet?"

Surely she was not in either of the rooms across the landing. She would have heard me if she had been.

Both doors stood ajar. "Dame Winet?" I called into the rooms.

She was not in either of them. We felt our way up the stairway to the third floor, and I called into the rooms there. Still she did not answer. Then we descended to the hall.

"Dame Winet? Are you here?" I called.

In answer my own voice bounced back at me from the walls. I stared about the room. It was lighter here because of the huge windows. I could make out the dim shape of chairs and a long table. But Dame Winet was not in the room. The entrance door stood open. Had she gone outside? In the middle of the night? She was certainly not in the castle.

Wolf grasped my cloak and tugged at it lightly.

"Yes, we must go, Wolf," I said to him. "We should never have come here. You were right: we should have gone on earlier. But we cannot leave now. We must tell Dame Winet what happened."

I pulled my cloak away from Wolf gently and sat down in a chair. Wolf stood facing me.

"We cannot leave her here all alone," I continued, "with that man lying dead in my room. Why did he come to my room, Wolf?"

I would have given almost anything if Wolf could have answered my question. But I felt certain that the man had come to harm me. Why else would he have crept in upon me like that? Wolf had known it, and he had killed the man before he could attack me.

I reached across and laid my hand on Wolf's head. He came to me and laid his head in my lap. I bent and kissed the top of it.

"Thank you, Wolf," I whispered. "Thank you, and forgive me for being cruel to you."

Wolf remained like that for some time, his head resting on my lap while I stroked him. Finally he sat down, leaning against me, and after a while he lay down by my ankle. In this way we waited for Dame Winet and the dawn.

I dozed finally, and when I woke, the night outside the windows had turned orange gray. I could see the hall clearly now in the morning light. It was sparsely furnished with three chairs and a long table that stood before the fireplace. Thick dust covered the table and the wooden trencher and broken goblet that lay upon it. Cobwebs formed graceful triangles between its top and legs. Spiders had webbed the chairs too and the corners of the walls. Dust covered everything—even the leaves which had floated in through the broken windows and lay scattered about the floor.

How utterly deserted and neglected the room looked. Now I noticed footprints in the dust and a trail brushed by Dame Winet's and my skirts leading across the room from the entrance door to the stairway. Surely no one lived here, I thought.

"Wolf," I said, "wake up. The good dame has not returned. We would have heard her if she had." I stood then and began to walk to the doorway. "Come along."

We climbed the stairway to the second floor and, pausing a moment outside the doorway to the room I had occupied, entered it. The dead man lay on his back beside the bed in a puddle of congealed brown blood. Blood lay spattered all about the floor. The ghastly wound at his throat was coated with it too, and so were his shoulders. The knight's stiff white hand clutched a dagger. He stared with dead, sightless eyes at the ceiling.

Sir Tor would pursue me no more. A great, black vulture sitting restlessly on the sill outside the window also knew he was dead. I turned almost at once away from the grisly sight, called Wolf away from the body, and left the room.

We climbed to the top floor and looked into the chambers there. They stood deserted and neglected. So did the chapel, one of the rooms opposite the chamber where Sir Tor lay.

But the long chamber beside the chapel was occupied. Someone slept on the bed there. I could not tell from the bones whether it had been a man or a woman. The dusty skeleton lay sprawled among shreds of cloth, feathers, and other debris. The hollow eyes of its gray-haired skull gazed toward a great hole in the window. Outside it the sky had turned blue.

We left the castle, and as we crossed the yard, I noticed that the door to the barn was latched from the outside. Then the sound of wings beating the air distracted me. I looked up at the window of the chamber where Sir Tor lay. The black bird hurled itself against the glass, shattering it. Then with a flurry of feathers it stepped through the window and disappeared into the room. Wolf and I turned and hurried toward the track and the road below the hill.

As we walked down it, I pieced together the fragments of the puzzle: Dame Winet did not live in the castle. No one had lived there for years—not since the owner had died alone in his bed.

Who was Dame Winet, then? What was her connection with Sir Tor? I asked her that when we found her waiting for us beside the wall where the track joined the road.

"Did you know Sir Tor Malafie, Dame Winet?" I asked.

"Sir Tor, dearie?" she said. "Who's Sir Tor? And did you have a comfy sleep? I have been out to see if I could find you something for breakfast. And here you are already up and away."

Wolf growled at the old woman and would have attacked her, I think, if I had not quieted him.

"Wolf!" I said. "Please! It seems you have had little success," I said to the woman.

"Not a thing, dearie."

"You do not know Sir Tor?"

"I never heard of him. Who is he?"

"You will find him waiting for you at the castle. You will be going back there, won't you? You will be going home?"

"Oh, yes. But you must run along now. You've a big day ahead. And it is fair, as I said it would be. But take care when you get to the fork in the road. Be sure to take the left road and not the right. The right goes where you don't want to go, dearie. Oh, mercy, no! Be sure to turn to the left. Remember, don't go to the right. It's the lefthand road you want to take."

I turned from her without another word and hurried away. Wolf ran ahead of me, and as we rounded a curve in the road, I glanced back. The old hag stood by the wall still, looking after us.

It would have been useless to have stayed and accused her of being Sir Tor's accomplice. She would only have denied it. But who Dame Winet was or why she had helped him did not matter. Sir Tor was dead and would not torment me further, and I would never see Dame Winet again.

So, despite the horror of the night before, it was with a light heart that Wolf and I walked along in the morning sunshine. We came to the fork in the road shortly before noon. Wolf took the road to the left, and when he had gone about thirty yards along it, he paused to wait for me.

"No, Wolf!" I called to him. "We will go this way."

I began to walk down the righthand road, but Wolf did not follow me.

"Come along, Wolf. Come! We cannot go that way. It would be foolish to."

Then I continued walking, losing sight of Wolf behind the trees. It was several minutes before I heard his feet patting the ground behind me, and then he brushed past me and stood before me as if to block my way.

"We cannot take Dame Winet's advice," I said to Wolf. "It is perfectly obvious that she wanted to harm me. I am sure that she directed us to the left because there is something unpleasant or dangerous there. No, Wolf, we will go this way and avoid whatever she wanted us to meet."

Our road was less traveled than the other. It wound through a deep oak wood. Beyond the wood the trees thinned and turned from oak to pine. And the soil, loamy beneath the oak trees, now became sandy, sparsely tufted with coarse grass among the clumps of trees. A little farther on we came to an area where a forest fire had reduced the trees to pointed black stumps and the grass to ashes.

This open devastation continued for miles, each aspect looking like the last. But then here and there puddles began to appear in the ground—small ones at first, soon becoming larger and more numerous. These had not, I felt, been left by the snow and sleet of the day before. They were not fresh like rain puddles, but were black, stagnant pools covered with oily, opalescent bubbles and gray-green slime. A haze hovered just above the surface of some of them.

These pools soon joined one another to form a morass. Now the water bubbled actively, exuding a fetid odor. The water steamed and the air grew warmer.

The torpid, vaporous mire stretched in an endless plain on either side of the road. It was broken only by a great hump of steaming, scale-covered rock, which jutted from a pool before us. Wolf was reluctant to approach it; he nosed my leg as we walked. But I hurried on, wanting only to leave the swamp behind.

The rock glistened with slime and smelled putrid. As we reached it, it uncoiled its long snakelike neck and swung its tiny head toward us. Slowly it raised its languid lids to gaze at us with yellow eyes. Its mouth gaped; a wreath of smoke drifted from it.

I ran! And as I fled, the thing shrieked with rage. A fiery blast hissed through the air behind me. I felt the heat of it on my neck. I glanced around at the beast. With a deafening roar it drew back its lips and spat a second stream of fire at me, scorching the road at my heels. I ran as fast as I could without looking back again until the cries of the monster had receded. Only then did I look around at it, transfixed.

The monster stood in the mire on its stubby legs, its long tail thrashing angrily. Wolf stood in the road facing the dragon and looking up at its head, which swung back and forth high above him. The beast spat its fiery breath at Wolf. Wolf leaped aside with the swiftness of a flickering shadow, and the flames missed their mark. Back and forth, back and forth, Wolf dodged as the monster spat at him, always escaping the blasts. And each time the dragon threw its fire, it lowered its head, drawing nearer to Wolf's body.

Finally, when the monster's head swung close above him, Wolf sprang at the dragon's throat. The beast screamed and whipped its head violently to throw Wolf off. But he gripped with his teeth and held on tightly. The dragon rubbed its throat against the ground. Wolf let go and sprang to earth. But before the dragon could pull away, he leaped again at its throat, rending it still further. Now the monster rolled on its back and thrashed, trying to fling Wolf away.

Wolf tore at the beast's throat repeatedly until even at that distance I could see the gaping wound and the green-orange fluid that gushed from it.

The dragon weakened; its movements slowed. With a mighty roar, it reared high into the air in one final paroxysm of rage. Then it crashed to earth and lay still.

I waited to see if the beast would move again. When it did not, I walked slowly to Wolf, who stood beside it. I crouched next to him and threw my arms around my friend. Wolf trembled, but he stood, tense and proud. Silently we gazed at Wolf's triumph. Then I rose and we walked away together.

We walked across the plain toward the mountains. By late afternoon, glowing orange and rose in the setting sun, they towered above us. And there, nestled in a lavender wood at their base, stood a cottage.

A woodsman and his wife lived there. They gave Wolf and me supper, invited us to sleep before their hearth, gave us breakfast in the morning and food to take with us.

I had been concerned about their reactions to Wolf. But I need not have been: they thought he was my dog. When they asked me why I called Wolf "Wolf" and I replied, "Because he looks so much like one," they seemed satisfied. And when I told them how Wolf had killed the dragon, they were overjoyed.

So we set out again, cheered by the woodsman's final remarks: that Tintagal lay at the end of the road on the other side of the mountains.

The road led gently upward, and the weather grew colder. Then on a still, pearl-gray morning, as we walked through brakes of hawthorn, it began to snow. Huge feathery flakes of it floated through the air and rested upon each delicate branch, twig, and thorn, turning the thickets to lace.

It was against one of these intricate snow tattings that a man stood quietly waiting for us.

Chapter Nineteen

✳✳✳✳✳✳✳✳✳✳✳✳✳✳✳✳✳✳✳

Elaine's Story

He was dressed in a voluminous yellow robe embroidered with pink peach blossoms. He was a frail, very old man, but despite his great age, his sallow skin remained smooth. His white beard and mustache, though sparse, reached nearly to his waist. But it was his eyes that interested me most, not only their peculiar slant and formation (their lids were entirely hidden as he looked at me), but the glint of amused tenderness that shone from them.

He carried a basket of flowers of every variety and color, it seemed. And as I reached him, he bowed and picked up a single pink rose—the kind that grew about Castle Idris by the thousands in June and July.

"It is lovely," I said. "We have them at home in the summer."

"It is for the lady," he said, holding it out to me.

"For me? I am sorry; I have nothing to give you for it."

"It is a gift, lady."

"How very kind of you." I took the rose and held it to my nose for a moment. Then I smiled at the man.

"Isn't it lovely? It is my favorite. Of all the flowers, I think I love this little rose more than any other. How can I thank you?"

The man did not answer, but he continued to gaze at me kindly.

"Why do you give it to me?" I asked.

He smiled. "It is for your dowry."

"My dowry?" I laughed gaily. "It would be most welcome as part of my dowry, reverend sir, if I were to have one, though I do not think it would be valued by anyone but me. But I do not plan to marry, so I need no dowry. May I keep the flower, even so?"

The man nodded.

"Then I shall wear it!" I said. "And have a journey the happier for it."

The old man turned from me and began to shuffle down the road in the direction we had come.

"Thank you for my rose," I called after him.

I stuck the stem of the flower through a link in the clasp of my cloak, and Wolf and I walked on.

We came to a hilltop during the afternoon and saw a village lying below us—a cluster of twenty or so rude cottages of clay and thatch. The village fields spread out around it in all directions, sloping up to the hills and forming a bowl-like valley. Our road led through the village, past its manor house beyond, and then up into the mountains again.

I was apprehensive about passing through the village with Wolf. But it was the only road. We had seen no other for hours. And after all, I thought, it was a tiny village. I could not see a soul about, and if anyone should happen to look out of a window as we passed by, he would surely think Wolf was a dog, just as the woodsman and his wife had done.

So, reassured somewhat by these thoughts, I walked with Wolf down the hill and into the village. But it did not remain deserted, as I had hoped. A woman appeared in the shadowy doorway of one of the cottages and stood staring at us.

Wolf growled at her.

At the same time the woman shrieked, "Wolf!" Then she screamed, "Wolf! Wolf! Wolf! It's come back! It's *here!* Come quick! Quick! Quick! The wolf! It's—"

With a snarl, Wolf darted across the road, sprang at the woman, and knocked her down. I ran to him to pull him away from the woman. But even before I reached him, the door to the adjoining cottage was thrown open, and a man dashed out of it brandishing a thick piece of firewood.

And then someone ran from one of the other houses shouting, "Wolf! Wolf!"

"Run, Wolf!" I shouted. *"Run!"*

Wolf leaped into the road and bolted down it toward the open fields. The two men ran after him, followed now by three or four other men, a couple of young boys, and several women. All these people had run out of their cottages with surprising speed, and all carried weapons of some kind—pokers, clubs, sticks, or canes. One man carried a spear. And all shouted, "Wolf! Wolf!" as they ran.

Wolf would outrun them easily, I thought. But then as Wolf reached the fields, my heart sank. Several men on horseback, preceded by a pack of baying dogs, rode from a fringe of trees in front of Wolf and galloped toward him. Wolf swerved in an oblique angle and shot across the field with the dogs and horsemen at his tail.

In a moment they vanished behind the row of houses, and I turned automatically to the woman on the ground beside me. But there was no one there. It had not taken Wolf half a minute to run out of sight. The woman could not have gotten up during that time and walked away: she would have brushed past me in that narrow doorway if she had.

Nevertheless she was gone. And as I looked bewilderedly about for her, a man limped across the road toward me.

"Where did she go?" I asked him.

"They'll get him this time," he said. "They'll get him. Proper lot of yelling you did, and a good thing too."

"I don't understand."

"It was you that seen him, wasn't it? It was you that shouted, wasn't it? Well?"

"But it wasn't me. It was a woman who— She stood right here. Did you see her?"

"I seen it all from my window there. There you was shouting and that creature running up the road."

"And you didn't see anyone else?"

"I seen everyone that came out to chase the beast."

"But there was a woman with me. With white hair. She had a wart on her chin and . . . "

The man was not interested. He turned away from me and hobbled up the road toward a small group of women and children who had gathered there to gaze out across the fields. But the group scattered even before he reached it; Wolf and his pursuers, then, were no longer visible.

Perhaps Wolf would escape. He must! If so, he would return to me. I was sure he would. Then I should stay in that valley so that he could find me.

I turned toward the manor house to seek hospitality for the night. As I walked toward it, I relived the events of the past few minutes. How quickly the men had run out of their cottages after Wolf. It was almost as though they had been waiting for him—almost as though it had all been planned.

And that woman: what had she meant by "It's come back"? I had sensed something familiar about her, even in those brief moments. I did not recognize her, but her voice had reminded me of someone else's. She had sounded like Dame Winet. But it could not have been Dame Winet's voice: Dame Winet had no wart on her chin.

Unexpectedly, the Lady De Fonêt at the manor house provided an answer to one of my questions. After I introduced myself, she told me that she and her husband, Sir Cedric, had known my father long ago.

Then she invited me to stay the night. And after explaining briefly, giving no details, that I was walking to Tintagal, and after we had talked for a few minutes, I asked about the woman in the village.

"You must know the villagers well," I said.

"Oh, yes. Each and every one," Dame De Fonêt said. "We look upon them rather as our children."

Then you must know an elderly white-haired woman with a wart on her chin. Who is she?"

Dame De Fonêt thought a moment and then said, "No. No, we have no one here like that. Dame Groote, our miller's wife, has white hair, but she has no wart on her chin. Why do you ask?"

"Because I spoke to the woman in the village."

"I wonder who she could be. A visitor, perhaps? But we should have known. That is rather odd. But then it has been such an odd— horrible, *horrible* day." She took a handkerchief from her sleeve and held it briefly to her mouth.

I looked at her inquiringly.

"We have had a tragedy. A horrible, gruesome tragedy. One of our dear little children—a little boy —was playing on the doorstep of his parent's cottage when a wolf came brazenly into the village and carried him off!

"The dogs found the child in the wood—horribly mangled and dead. The poor little body was still warm. My husband and every knight and gentleman and everyone who has a horse has been out ever since hunting down the beast. The child was screaming in terror as he was carried away, and the wolf was seen. It was a huge, ugly black wolf—all alone. It came—"

"No, that is impossible," I said. "He was with me."

"With you? Who was with you, my dear?"

"Ah— God in heaven. And he was surely with that little boy."

That had been a terribly lame reply, and I wondered if Dame De Fonêt had thought it peculiar. She had, I found out later.

Chapter Twenty

✸✸✸✸✸✸✸✸✸✸✸✸✸✸✸✸✸✸✸

Elaine's Story

I heard Dame De Fonêt and her husband talking in their chamber as I walked down to the hall for supper that night. Since they spoke of me, I stopped and listened.

"His daughter?" Sir Cedric asked.

"Yes," Dame De Fonêt replied. "And do you know, she said the strangest thing. She said that she had talked to her father *recently*."

"Impossible! The man has been dead for ten years or more. And you say she is alone? No attendants? Nobody? *Walking*?"

"Yes. And dressed in the most . . . ordinary—"

"It is certainly not she. The Lady Elaine has only just returned to Castle Idris. She had been at a convent, I believe. Prior Benedict told me. He had just visited Castle Idris. He should know. And are we not attending her marriage to Prince John and all the festivities? What does she look like?"

"Slender, pretty, lovely golden hair. She was wearing a green cloak."

"The girl in the village," he said.

"Which girl in the village?" Dame De Fonêt asked.

"The girl who saw the wolf again. The girl who shouted the alarm."

"It came back? Again? Oh, Cedric, no! How *horrible!* Did you get it?"

"Sir Hugh wounded it—in the rump. Blood all over the place. We lost it down by the river. But it cannot live long, bleeding like that. It will crawl into a cave somewhere and die. We are rid of the thing."

"Strange she did not mention it. And she said the most peculiar thing. I told her about the little Grevel child, naturally, and after I had described the brute, she said, 'That is not possible. He was with me.' "

"Didn't you ask her what she meant?"

"Yes. She said something about God, but that was not what she had meant at all."

"I don't like it. We shall have to get rid of her."

"But we *can't!* She seems highborn, whoever she is. Surely she can stay the night, and then tomorrow . . . "

I did not wait to hear more.

That evening, then, I was not seated at the high table. I sat just below it. My dinner companion was a pleasant enough young man named Sir Philip. Across from me sat Sir Hugh.

It was a distressing meal. First Sir Hugh explained in detail how he had wounded Wolf. I do not wish to repeat what he said; even now it causes me too much anguish. But he was sure my friend was dead.

"Did you see him die?" I said.

"No, he got away in the river," Sir Hugh said. "Swam under the water, I suppose. But he could not live with a wound like that. Maybe he has drowned."

"Maybe Thod will get him," Sir Philip said. "They would deserve each other."

"He would not be interested," Sir Hugh said. "Our cattle would be more to his liking. Or one of us."

"They have left Bouton, you know," Sir Philip said. "Gone down to Burleigh."

"Thod? Bouton?" I asked.

"The giant," Sir Philip said to me. "Don't you know about Thod?"

"No. No, but I heard there was a giant living in the mountains."

"And preying on every living thing for twenty miles around. Hugh, we must do something."

"What would you suggest?" Sir Hugh said.

"Get an army."

"How could an arrow pierce his skin?" Sir Hugh asked. "He would stomp us to death and laugh while he did it—the stupid, ugly brute. That cottage in Bouton was smashed to splinters and four people eaten and their bones ground up for flour, more than likely. No wonder the rest have gone to Burleigh. So would I. And we may be next."

They went on talking about the giant and describing how various people had seen his enormous hulk stalking about the mountains. And they explained how he liked best to eat people and how he had begun to forage farther and farther abroad. I was glad when the meal was over and I could retire to my chamber.

The following morning the church bell began to toll as I left the manor house to walk to the village. I passed the cemetery and a freshly dug grave there. Then a little farther on, a group of black-garbed figures trudged down the road through patches of dirty snow toward me. They followed a little coffin of freshly sawed wood and a woman weeping.

I stood aside and watched the procession pass, looking for a white-haired woman with a wart on her chin. But I did not see her, and wished that I had not been there to endure the sullen, suspicious glances of the mourners.

I walked on, and when I reached the village, I asked a youth who lounged outside the alewife's house if he knew an old woman with a wart on her chin. He looked at me as though I were demented and said he did not.

I left him and walked on past the village and up the hill. There was no hurry: I had begged to stay one more night at the manor house, and my request had been granted, though somewhat grudgingly, I thought.

All that day I walked so that if Wolf was anywhere about, he could meet me in any number of secluded places. But he did not appear.

The next day after our morning bread and watered wine, I thanked my host and hostess, left the manor house, and walked toward Tintagal.

Why did I go to Tintagal, especially now that I was all alone? Prince John was to marry my stepsister. He would scarcely be glad to see me. But what else could I do? At least if I walked to Tintagal, I would be doing something. I could not do nothing.

And Wolf—poor Wolf. Did he lie dying in a cave somewhere, or was he dead already? Tears blurred my sight as I thought of him.

My arm brushed the purse at my girdle. In it lay the blue glass bottle. Should I carry it with me any farther? It seemed that I would have tears enough of my own. It was a pretty color, though: I would keep it awhile longer. Then I bent my head to smell the rose at my throat. A tear fell upon it and lay, a sparkling orb, on one of its petals.

How strange it was to smell its fragrance there in the wintry mountains, those great crags thrusting their slabs at the sky. All day I plodded through them. It was a frighteningly wild and deserted place of frozen snow patches, pine trees, and stone.

Yet, as I had so many times since meeting Dame Winet, and even before, I felt that someone was watching me. Today I had felt it ever since leaving the manor house in the morning. Late in the afternoon, I suddenly was overwhelmed by the sensation, but it was different now, palpable and immediate.

I looked over my shoulder, never expecting to see

anyone. But I did: a huge head and shoulders rose from behind a rocky hummock. I was so dumbfounded that it was a moment before I could move. Then I darted headlong into a thicket of pine saplings beside the road. The young trees were taller than I, and bushy. I stood still, hardly breathing, watching from among the branches.

The giant, dressed in a crude sleeveless fur garment, climbed the rocky slope, finally standing on the crest of it. He bent over, his hands on his knees, and stared intently down at the road.

That the figure was Thod, I had no doubt. He was not as immense as I had imagined. His height had, I supposed, been exaggerated as stories about him had been told and retold. Nevertheless, he was a terrifying apparition. I judged him to be twelve or fourteen feet tall. He was thickly proportioned, muscular, with huge hands, and a tiny, almost chinless head capping a trunklike neck. His lips were thick and fleshy, his eyes glassy and vacuous under heavy lids.

Had he seen me? I did not know how excellent his sight was, so I could not judge. But even if he saw well, he might not have noticed me at the side of the road among the long shadows of the rocks and trees.

Now he shambled down the slope toward me, staring at the clump of trees in which I stood and uttering a deep, broken, growl-like moan.

I ran when he was almost upon me. I felt certain then that he had seen me run into the trees and that he was coming to grab me. I left my cover and dashed down an open grassy slope toward a wood of pine below me. Once inside the wood the spongy ground tilted steeply downward, and I ran between the trees so swiftly that I was unable to keep from tumbling over a precipice. I did not fall far, however: it was not a very tall cliff. And I landed without injury on a cushion of pine needles.

I crouched there, hidden from Thod at the base of the bluff, listening for him. And I thanked God for my hiding place and for the southerly slope down which I had fled. It must have been a southerly one because the snow had melted almost entirely away, eliminating the danger of telltale footprints.

But Thod needed no footprints to tell him the direction I had taken: he had seen me run across the open meadow from the clump of pines. Now he came after me. Branches splintered before his advance, and entire trees crashed to the ground. The havoc above me seemed to shake the very cliff against which I cowered.

Shortly, however, the noise seemed less loud. It became apparent that Thod no longer strode toward me but had swerved and now trod down the mountainside obliquely away from me. Then the noise stopped altogether. He was gone.

Nevertheless, I did not move but strained my ears listening for his sounds. I thought I heard a stone strike another. Was that the scrape of a boot on the rocks? Yes, it was. Then I heard several footsteps and cracking branches once again. He was coming back, but this time he approached from below me.

He drew steadily nearer as I crouched there, fixed with terror. Surely he would see me, coming from that direction. I must run. Looking frantically about, I noticed that the cliff turned a sharp corner about ten yards away. I jumped to my feet and ran around it. There, down a short slope, gaped a fissure in the rock. Thod was almost upon me now; the noise was deafening. I ran to the shallow cave and crawled into it. It was dry and dark there. He could not possibly see me.

But then my heart missed a beat. Looking out at the slope I had just crossed, I saw my footprints: their black shadows spotted the patch of snow that lay there still.

Chapter Twenty-one

✳✳✳✳✳✳✳✳✳✳✳✳✳✳✳✳✳✳✳✳✳

Gloria's Story

Late in the same afternoon that we had acquired the chest of jewels, Prince John's clothes were found by the seashore beneath the castle's outer wall. They lay not far from the postern. Prince John had gone swimming before supper and had drowned. The body of a man, horribly mutilated by some sea monster, was washed up days later on the shore several miles along the coast from Castle Idris. It could only have been John's. It was sent to his father in Tintagal for burial.

Mother assured me that Prince John's death did not matter. I would marry William, who now became heir to the throne. I felt no remorse over John's death; indeed, I was pleased about it. I would never forget the look of revulsion on his face when he had met me, and I would never have forgiven him for it. I could not have been content with such a man.

But suppose William was already betrothed? This we learned later had been so, but fortunately William's betrothed died of a mysterious malady the day after John had drowned. So, as Mother had predicted, it was agreed that William would marry me. And since preparations had long been under way in Tintagal for John's marriage, William's would now take place on that same day.

As Mother had also predicted, winter came early to Castle Idris that year; soon ice covered the fish pool on many days. It was too cold to sit on its rim on those days. Sometimes, however, the ice melted. Then Mother would sit there and daydream as she gazed into the water.

But though my future was assured, and if Prince William should prove to be less willful than his brother, Mother's was, too, she was not content. She was ill at ease and irritable.

A fine snow had begun to fall one afternoon as Mother had paced the garden walks. I hated snow and I hated that frigid castle. It was like living in an ice-house. And I loathed the melancholy mood Mother had drawn about us. I determined to find out once and for all what was annoying her, and to put an end to it. So I threw on my warmest cloak, went into the courtyard, and demanded to know what was the matter. She evaded my questions with jumbled nonsense.

As she spoke, I felt that we were not alone. I turned and saw behind us the most appalling old man. He must have come through the archway. He was dressed in a long yellow robe that was magnificently embroidered. I wondered how such a repellent creature could be so richly dressed. His skin was sallow, almost yellow. His slanted eyes had no lids. And his long bony fingers wore nails several inches long.

Most peculiar of all, he carried a basket of flowers. And without a word this utter stranger had the effrontery to offer me a rose from his basket. It was an ordinary pink rose, the kind that grew wild about the castle by the thousands in June. I told him that I did not want it, that it was common. Who was he, I asked, and what was he doing at the castle? He did not answer me, but with an evil smile he offered me another flower. I think it was a carnation. It was also common: many carnations grew in the castle's gardens in summer.

The man seemed determined, however, to thrust a flower upon me. If I was to put an end to this indignity and be rid of him, I supposed I had to accept one. But if that was so, it must be a flower that suited my station. I was the daughter of the Duke of Idris and not some lowborn peasant girl. I told the stranger this. He offered me several other flowers, each more exotic-looking than the last. I refused them all, asking for one more splendid still.

At last he held a curious flower out to me and told me that it was the finest he possessed. It was the only flower of its kind that had ever existed. Its petals and leaves were carved from the rarest pink and green jade. Surely this was the most sumptuous flower in all the world and fitting for such a personage as myself.

This mollified me somewhat. I accepted the flower and told the man to go to the hall where someone would show him where to eat and a cell in which to sleep.

Mother and I examined the flower. It was most beautifully made—almost lifelike. Mother decided that it would join the queen's treasure as part of my dowry.

Though I did not know it then, my dowry was not yet complete: further good fortune awaited along the road to Tintagal. We were to stay at the palace there until the marriage. So we left Castle Idris late in December with an escort of fifty gentlemen and yeomen, all armed in case of attack by bandits. I had refused to ride a mule all the way to Tintagal, so Mother and I traveled in a horse litter in the center of the procession.

On the afternoon of the third day, the boredom of the journey was alleviated by a sudden halt. We were then in a seemingly endless wood, far from a village or habitation of any kind.

We had stopped because something unusual had been discovered beside the road. Of course I got out of the litter and went to see what it was. A richly dressed man lay there. He was all alone. He had been wounded and was bleeding from the side—his cloak was red with blood. And he had been cut about the forehead.

I suppose he could tell by my appearance that I was the lady of the party, for he spoke only to me. He said that he had been attacked by bandits and badly wounded. He begged me to help him, saying that he would die if I did not. Then he held out his purse to me and said that I could have all it contained if I would bind his wound and take him with me to the nearest inn.

I took the purse and told the man that there was no one in the party who could tend him; that we were in a great hurry; and that we had no spare horse or mule on which to carry him. But we would inform someone at the nearest inn of his plight and send them back to fetch him.

Then I directed our party to proceed at once and rejoined Mother in the litter. As we marched on, I told her what had happened and that it would have been dangerous to have remained there. The man may have been a trap set by bandits to cause us to stop. Or he may have been diseased: we could certainly not risk becoming ill. And it was obvious that he was dying anyway, so it was just as well to leave him behind and forget all about him.

I hoped the man's purse would contain sufficient recompense for having encountered such a repellent incident. On opening it, Mother and I discovered that it contained thirty silver deniers.

These became the third part of my dowry. It was now a very rich dowry indeed. King Alfred would be delighted. He could not possibly have found anyone with as much wealth to bring Prince William as I. In fact, it was far too rich a dowry, and I suggested to Mother that we keep part of it for ourselves. But she said that once I was married to William, I should demand that he care for both of us as was befitting and that we would thereby get the value of it back and more besides.

So in spite of Elaine, and Prince John, and Merlin, and everything that had seemed at first to interfere with Mother's and my plan, it had all turned out perfectly. I would soon be Princess Elaine, and in the near future, Queen Elaine. I could not help wishing still that Tintagal were a larger kingdom. I deserved something better, but I supposed I should have quite an agreeable future there, nevertheless.

I shall be much too busy being princess and queen to continue this narrative. And there would be no purpose in doing so, since the story is actually finished: the heroine marries the wealthy prince and lives contentedly ever after.

The End of Gloria's Story

Chapter Twenty-two

❈❈❈❈❈❈❈❈❈❈❈❈❈❈❈❈❈❈❈

Elaine's Story

Perhaps Thod would not see the footprints leading to me. Perhaps he would go around the other side of the bluff, or perhaps he would simply step straight up it. The air was still now. He must have stopped walking to look about. Then I heard the thud of his footsteps. A tree snapped and crashed to the ground. Then the wood was quiet again.

But though I heard no sound, Thod moved; a wide shadow crossed the patch of snow before me. He had leaned over the cliff to see what was around the corner. I faced the wall and pressed myself against it, covering my face with my hands. I could not look. I heard his high-pitched growling moan, his footsteps grew louder, and then two enormous hands gripped my waist and lifted me into the light.

Thod held me at arm's length to examine me.

"Please!" I cried. "Put me down! Let me go! My father is the Duke of Idris. He will . . . "

I did not struggle because, held high above the ground like that, I feared I might fall. Nor did I con-

tinue my plea. In spite of my terror, I had examined
Thod as he had examined me. He was a dolt. His in-
flamed eyes held not a spark of keenness nor intelligence. They were glassy and dull. I would never be
able to reason with him. I was not even sure that he
would understand what I said. Even if I should try,
he would pay no attention: the spittle which flowed
from the corner of his open mouth proclaimed his in-
tentions.

He flung me over his shoulder and, holding me
tightly by the waist with both hands, stalked toward
the setting sun.

I had no idea how long he carried me—whether it
was ten minutes or three quarters of an hour. His
shoulder bruised my ribs and stomach almost at once,
and my neck and head ached from being tossed violently from side to side as with huge strides Thod
strode through the mountains. I fainted, regained con-
sciousness, and fainted again.

Finally I became dimly aware that he had slowed
his pace. We passed through a doorway. Now alert, I
smelled meat cooking. Smoke smarted my eyes. Thod
shut a door behind us. He took a key which hung by
a thong from a nail beside the door, carried me across
the room, thrust me into what seemed to be a cage,
slammed its door shut, locked it, and put the key on
a shelf or ledge somewhere above me.

Then he walked to a rude table, threw himself into
a chair, and growled loudly. He did not growl at me,
he growled at another figure almost as large as he who
worked over a fire in the center of the hut. It seemed
to be a woman. She lifted a huge carcass, probably
a cow, from the fire, the spit still skewering it, and
plopped it on the table.

Then she sat down opposite Thod. He had already
torn a leg from the animal and, clutching it in his
hands, had begun to eat it. The giantess tore off a
piece too and handed it to a giant child who sat on
the floor by her chair.

While they ate, paying no attention to me, I studied

my surroundings. The house consisted of one long room. The building was made of stones and was similar to the turf huts which were common in the countryside around Castle Idris. The end walls were perpendicular, while the side walls leaned gradually toward each other and finally met, forming the roof. A hole in the center of the roof allowed some smoke to escape and, when the door was closed, lighted the room, since there were no windows. Little light shone through it now, though, as it was almost dark outside.

Inside, the wood fire burned brightly, reflecting on the greasy mouths and hands of the three diners as they devoured the roasted animal. And it lit enough of the room for me to see the few objects it contained: the skinned carcass of a sheep hanging from the roof, a wide mound of hay covered with a patchwork of furs sewn together, a pile of logs, some pots and other cooking utensils, and my cage standing against the wall beside an empty one just like it. The earthen floor was strewn with bones, scraps of hide, bits of wood, and other debris. The air smelled of wood smoke, cooked meat, rancid fat, and filth.

My cage was made of iron bars and had a wooden floor. I had seen cages like it many times: trained bears were carried in them from manor house to castle to village fair. I was able to stand upright in mine and walk two paces in each direction.

The giant and his wife ignored me completely. After they had finished eating, leaving the bones of their supper on the table top, they lay down in the corner to sleep. The child, larger in size than I, meandered to my cage, looked intently at me for a few moments, and then lay down beside her parents. Soon all three slept.

I did not. At least I do not think I did. I watched the fire die, listened to the giants snore, and waited for the dawn. And I cursed fate for arranging my meeting with Thod.

But it had not been fate that had arranged it. I learned this as I watched the child play the following morning. I think it was a girl. She was perhaps six inches taller than I, but her head and hands were twice the size of mine. She had slept for hours, though Thod had left the house soon after daylight. When she finally wakened, she got up and wandered about aimlessly, chewing on a bone which she found on the table. Then she discovered a piece of paper on the floor.

She looked at it, then glanced sideways at me, then studied the paper, pretending exaggerated interest in it. She threw it into the air, and as it floated down she tried to catch it. Over and over she repeated the process, glancing at me occasionally to see if I was watching. Suddenly, holding the paper out for me to see, she rushed at my cage, but as she drew near she swung it behind her back out of sight.

She did this several times until finally I turned my back on her. I refused to be the object of her teasing. But then she moaned pathetically and I turned around. She stood almost against the bars of the cage, grinning stupidly at me and holding up the piece of paper for me to see.

On it an amateurish and much-worked-over drawing pictured a girl walking along a road through mountains toward a distant city. Under the drawing this short poem was printed:

> *Along the road on pretty feet*
> *Walks a damsel tender and sweet.*
> *She walks to Tintagal today.*
> *Catch her and carry her away.*

"Did you do that?" I asked the child, pointing at the drawing. "It is really very good."

The child looked at me, bewildered.

"You are really very clever to have done it so well. And did you write that lovely poem?"

Suddenly the girl swung about and danced away, flinging the paper into the air. She danced around and around the fire, laughing. It was a mindless laugh. She was an imbecilic creature: she had not understood a

word I had said and hadn't the faintest idea what the
words on the paper meant, though she might have
understood the drawing and related it to me.

That the girl in the drawing was meant to be me, I
was certain. The damsel in the poem referred to me
too. But that idiotic child had not created either, nor
had Thod. He was incapable of it. Had his wife?

The giantess sat staring vacantly at the fire as her
daughter danced round and round it, laughing and
screaming. Finally she stood, and when the child approached, she stepped forward and cuffed her hard
on the side of the head. The child bellowed, ran to
the bed, threw herself down on it, curled into a ball,
and was silent.

"Did *you* write that poem?" I called to the woman
after a moment. "Dame Thod? Dame Thod? Did you
write that lovely poem?"

The giantess walked back to her chair, glanced at
me with little interest, and then looked away. She said
nothing, and I was sure she had not understood what
I had said. She was as ignorant as her husband.

The woman continued to ignore me, but the child
was as fascinated by me as her mother was uninter-
ested. And when her mother left the house during the
afternoon, she got up from the bed and again danced
wildly around the fire, glancing at me now and then
as she did so. Then she ran to a corner where several
long wooden poles stood, grasped one by its end as
though it were a sword, rushed at me, and would have
thrust it into me if I had not dodged quickly aside.

She retreated and again lunged at me with the pole.
Again I dodged it. I was evidently something to play
with, and the game that afternoon was to be Run the
Pole through the Girl in the Cage. Again and again I
sidestepped her weapon, but soon, with fatigue, she
became annoyed and no longer lunged at me; she
stood still outside the cage thrusting the pole at me
with rapid, vicious jabs. Terrified, I danced back and
forth to avoid them.

Then, just in time, the door flew open and the

giantess entered the house. She saw what was happening, strode to her daughter, and struck her on the head—this time even harder than before. The child fell to the floor, dropping the pole. Then she crawled shrieking to the bed, pulled the furs over her head and lay still.

After that the woman took down the carcass of the sheep, spitted it and roasted it over the fire. It was cooked by the time Thod returned. He came home empty-handed that night. As soon as he arrived, the family devoured the sheep as they had the cow the night before. And as they had the night before, all three ignored me as they ate.

But that night when Thod had finished his supper, he gazed for several moments at the hook from which the carcass of the sheep had hung, and then he looked at me. The expression on his face was terrifying.

Chapter Twenty-three

****

Elaine's Story

After Thod and his wife had lain down that night, the child grasped a large knife from among some pots on the floor and crept across the room to me. With an imaginary steel, she pretended to sharpen the knife. Then after feeling the blade with her thumb, she drew the knife horizontally through the air in front of her throat while bulging her eyes at me.

Long after the giants slept, I sat huddled in my cloak on the floor of my cage, thinking. I was not surprised at my fate. I had known from the moment Thod had captured me that I would be killed and eaten.

When would they do it? Tomorrow? Would Thod kill me or would the giantess do it? Whoever did would probably cut my throat. Would it hurt?

It would be quick, I supposed. I did not mind dying so much, though I was terrified of the pain. No, it was not death that filled me with despair, it was the fact that I had experienced so little joy in life. I felt cheated. And the end would be so ghastly.

Wolf had died in an ugly manner too, pursued by dogs and strangers, wounded horribly, and finally crawling off to die slowly and alone.

Life should not end that way, I thought. And it should be more than tending swine, and being cold at night, and dying in this filthy hut at the hands of one of those monsters.

"Life should be more than that," I whispered aloud. "Shouldn't it?"

"Of course it should," a woman's voice said. "Wolf is not dead, and you will not be, either—at least not for a long time."

Did a tiny old woman with white hair actually stand beside me inside my cage? Was I dreaming? She was terribly bony and bent, with a large head and hands like the claws of a bird. Her eyes sparkled in the fire's glow, and she smiled at me.

"Wolf is not dead?" I asked. "How do you know that?"

"Because I saw him not ten minutes ago. He is quite alive."

"Shhh! They will hear you."

"They will sleep until morning. The end of the world would not wake them."

I stood and faced her. "Who are you?" I asked. "How did you get in here?"

The woman chuckled. "I am your godmother."

"I did not know I had a godmother."

"Everyone has a godmother. But most people never need her. They can usually take care of themselves. And if they did need her, they would not detain her with chatter. Especially after she had come to this disgusting hovel. The odor is *unbearable!*" She shut her eyes and grimaced. "Now, you must leave here at once. You have a long way to go before morning. If *you* don't want to, *I* do."

"I can't!" I said. "I am locked in here."

"Then you must unlock yourself."

"But I have no key."

Godmother glanced at the sleeping giants. "I do

not mind stupidity, but when it threatens the lives of intelligent people by its sheer brutal power, it is time to intervene. There is too much of that kind of thing abroad in the world, and it is time for thinking people to take a stand against it. Do something, child! Use your *intelligence!*"

"What do you want me to do?"

"Get the key and unlock the door of this cage so that you can walk out of it. I could do it for you, but I won't. I am extremely good at making things move by themselves, though." She smiled broadly at me. "Wineglasses, for instance."

"Was it *you?* Why? Why did you do it?"

"Because it was necessary. But you will learn all about that later. I shall not remain in this place long enough to explain, and neither will you. Now, think! Think!

"I *am* thinking."

"You are not thinking hard enough." Godmother pointed to the wall above us. "What is that hanging over that flat rock?"

"It is the thong attached to the key. But I cannot reach it. I have tried."

"You *can* reach it. What is that?"

"The pole that awful child tormented me with this afternoon."

"Can you reach *it?*"

"Yes, I think so."

I reached out and grasped the pole, and as I did so, I realized that I should have tried to escape long before Godmother had appeared.

"How stupid of me!" I said.

I stuck the pole up between the bars of the cage and raised it until the end of it passed through the loop of the thong. Then by tilting the pole, I pulled the key off its rocky shelf, and it slid by its thong down the pole into my hand.

"Well," Godmother sighed. "You see?"

Grasping the key, I reached through the bars of the cage, inserted the key in the lock, twisted it, and

pushed the door open. Then I left the cage and Godmother followed me. We walked across the room, past
the sleeping giants, and out of the house, closing the
door tightly behind us.

"Now go," Godmother said. "You have a long
walk. Follow that path there, and it will take you to
the Tintagal road. The moon will light your way. Do
you think you can find the cave where the giant captured you?"

"I think so, once I reach the road."

"Then go there. You will need to rest, and you
should arrive at—just about daybreak, I should think.
There is one thing that I must caution you about. Do
not under any circumstances travel by daylight. This
is *very* important, it would be *dangerous* for you to do
so. Remain in the cave all day tomorrow. Then travel
by night. Hide yourself during the days thereafter
under a ledge, or in a cave, or under thick pine trees
—anywhere where you could not possible be seen.
Do you understand that?"

"Yes. But where shall I go?" I asked.

"Go to Tintagal as you had planned, and find
Merlin."

"Merlin?"

"Merlin, the magician."

"But I don't know him."

"You do not need to know someone in order to
find him."

I looked down the path which Godmother had
pointed to. "But where is Wolf? Will I see him
again?"

She did not answer me. I turned back to her, but
she was gone.

I hurried away from the giant's house along the
path that Godmother had shown me. It was one of
Thod's paths, and in many places his long stride had
allowed him to step across a crevasse or up a bluff
which I had to find my way around. So the distance
that Thod had traversed in three quarters of an hour
or less took me the entire night. And as Godmother

had predicted, I arrived at the road to Tintagal as the eastern sky began to lighten.

I judged that I should turn south to find the clump of trees in which I had hidden from Thod, and I was right. After I had located them, it was easy to find my way across the clearing to the wood, through the trees to the cliff, and around the corner of it to the cave.

As I approached it, I was careful to step in the footprints I had made in the snow two days before. I looked toward the gaping hole in the rock and thought I saw a movement there.

Chapter Twenty-four

✵✵✵✵✵✵✵✵✵✵✵✵✵✵✵✵✵✵✵✵✵

Elaine's Story

It was too dark inside it to see. But then I heard a whine, and Wolf came out of the cave to greet me. He limped slowly, painfully toward me. I forgot all about the footprints then and ran to him. Falling on my knees before him, I threw my arms about his neck and hugged him tightly as he licked my face.

"Did you follow me?" I asked, holding him away from me.

Wolf beat his tail in the snow.

"Dear Wolf. You are terribly hurt, aren't you? Here, let me see."

I tried to turn Wolf so that I could see his rear leg, but he seemed to know what I wanted and did not wish me to look at it. Finally, though, he allowed me to examine the wound. It was a horribly deep gash that looked as if it had been made by a spear. The flesh was torn for six inches across his hip, and all around it the hair was matted and crusted with dried blood.

"Does it hurt very much? But it does look as though

it is healing. There is no festering. We will rest today and that should do it good. Come into the cave out of the wind."

But Wolf did not want to rest. Instead he tried persistently to lead me back toward the road to Tintagal. Finally I told him that I had not slept for two nights, and he followed me reluctantly into the cave. And when I told him about the giants and what Godmother had said, he seemed to acquiesce completely.

"So we will stay here and rest until dark," I said. I lay curled up comfortably on a bank of pine needles. Wolf lay close beside me. And the rose at my throat perfumed the air about us. "Then we will go on to Tintagal by night, and try to find a man—a magician, Godmother said—whose name is Merlin. He will—"

Wolf whined and beat his tail on the ground frantically.

"One would almost think you knew him. He will help us, I suppose. Otherwise Godmother would not have told me to find him." Suddenly I was very sleepy. "I . . . I cannot help but wonder if . . . Godmother was really there or . . . whether I dreamed it."

I slept.

We walked all that next night. Wolf's wound pained him terribly and forced him to walk very slowly. I felt unbearably sorry for him as he limped along the road, and when he looked up at me as if to say, "I am sorry to hold us back like this, but I cannot go any faster," I almost cried.

He would not rest until dawn, though I tried to convince him to stop hours before that. So when the sky began to lighten, we found a dry, hidden place beside a stream under a stone bridge. We slept the day there and walked on after dark.

The snow had all melted away now. The road was dry and hard. The nights were cold, but they were invigorating rather than uncomfortable. How beautifully the stars lay scattered across the black sky, like snow sparkles cast upon velvet.

We walked at night without seeing anyone, though once we did pass a track leading off into the trees where a sign swung on a post, and a little later we saw the lights of an inn. But we did not dare go there: I had no money and I was afraid for Wolf's safety.

Then one morning as the air about us lightened to gray and we began to search for a place to spend the day, I heard a faint cry from somewhere ahead of us. At first I thought it must be an animal, but when I heard it a second time, I feared it was a person crying out in pain. I hurried down the road, leaving Wolf to follow at his own speed.

It was a person, I discovered. A man lay all alone on the barren, sandy roadside He might have been thirty-three or thirty-five-years old and was richly dressed in a long brocaded coat lined with miniver, and in beautiful boots and soft leather gloves. He was wounded; blood had soaked through his coat, staining it scarlet in a wide area at his side, and he had been cut all about the forehead as though with pricking jabs of a knife or dagger.

"Help me!" the man called weakly to me.

I ran to him and knelt by his side.

"Bandits!" he murmured. "I— Help me! I am wounded. I will die if you don't." He lifted his purse from among the folds of his coat. "I will pay you. Take it! Take it all! Only bind my wound and help me to an inn."

"Of course I will help you," I said to the man, "but I cannot take your money for it."

I stood and gazed frantically about. What should I do? Could there be someone nearby to help? No, that was wishful thinking: we were far from anyone. I would have to do it myself. But I did not know how, I thought in panic. Then I remembered the way Brian had bound the would in Sir Tor's shoulder.

Kneeling beside the man, I took my knife from

its scabbard and slit his coat down the front. Then I peeled it quickly aside, unfastened his belt, and with the man's help, drew his tunic high up around his chest, baring his woolen shirt and drawers. His long shirt was of fine wool and, once slit with my knife, tore easily. I stripped it from his body and, as quickly as I could, made a pad and tore the remainder into strips. Then I pressed the pad to the bleeding gash in the man's side and wound the strips of cloth tightly about him.

Wolf arrived as I finished. He did not seem to surprise or disturb the man. Instead he sat up with rather remarkable strength, I thought, and then staggered to his feet.

"I don't think you should," I said. "You will make it bleed."

As I spoke, I noticed that the sun had already bathed the sky orange and that the orange had begun to fade. I remembered what Godmother had told me. Wolf and I should be in hiding now. But I could not run off and leave a wounded man alone. I must help him, and if somehow or other I risked danger by being out in the light, I would have to do so.

The man took a faltering step toward the road and would have fallen, I think, if I had not stepped quickly to his side so that he could hold onto me.

"Help me," he murmured.

He put his arm about my neck and drew me forward with him as he took another step, and another, and then another. He was heavy, and I was sure we could not go very far that way, but perhaps I could help him to the turn in the road. There we might see some habitation. But the road stretched on with no sign of a living soul.

I was soon exhausted and was about to tell the man that I could not go on in that manner any longer when I heard the distant sound of horses' hoofs behind us.

"Listen!" I said. "Riders are coming. They will take you to an inn."

We walked to a fallen tree a few yards from the roadside and sat down on it to wait. Wolf lay down at my feet.

The party sounded like a large one, and they were coming fast. But we had heard not only the horsemen that approached from behind us; twelve horsemen also rode toward us from the other direction. They arrived first. I stiffened, thinking the bandits had returned, but then I noticed that each man wore an identical purple coat and the same badge on his shoulder.

"They are my friends," the man said. "They have come to find me."

The men dismounted and stood in a semicircle in front of us as they greeted the wounded man. He told them how I had helped him, and assured his friends that he could return with them to his mansion.

While all this was going on, the procession coming from the other direction passed us. Fortunately Wolf, the wounded stranger, and I were hidden from it by his friends and their horses. It was fortunate because the procession had come from Castle Idris. I caught glimpses of several gentlemen whom I recognized and of the Idris badge that they wore. And I also saw a litter in which, I supposed, rode my stepmother and stepsister. I was still afraid that my stepmother would punish me for having stabbed Sir Tor, and I wanted nothing more to do with her or Gloria. So I breathed a sigh of relief when they and their party had passed out of sight.

I turned to the wounded man to bid him goodbye.

"Take this," he said, handing me his purse.

"No, I couldn't," I replied.

He reached into his purse then. By the way he held it, I could tell that it was almost empty. This surprised me, but when he drew a piece of rusty metal from it and handed it to me, I was more surprised still.

"Take this in remembrance of me," he said.

I took the object and examined it. It was about six inches long, square, and tapered from a flanged end almost to a point.

"What is it?" I asked him. "It looks like a nail."

"It is a nail," he said. "It is for your dowry."

"Thank you," I said. "I do not think I shall need a dowry, but I—I shall keep it as a remembrance."

Then I said goodbye, and Wolf and I walked away down the road to Tintagal.

Soon we saw the ruins of an ancient stone tower rising above the trees. We left the road and walked through the wood to it, but it was not deserted, as I had hoped.

Chapter Twenty-five

✛✛✛✛✛✛✛✛✛✛✛✛✛✛✛✛✛✛✛

Elaine's Story

A hermit had taken up residence in it. He was a kind old man. He gave us food and water, and allowed us to spend the day hiding in the tower.

But first I climbed the stairs to the top to see the view. From the tower the mountain sloped away to a broad valley, and there before the cliffs that edged the sea stood a city. I looked down at last on the plains of Tintagal and the sea that washed the Irish shores.

At our slow pace the city appeared to be a night's journey away, and it was. At sunrise the following morning we stood on a hill above it. Our road descended the hill and ran across a wide, level meadow to the city wall. A tournament was to be held in the meadow; a fence of stake enclosing an oblong field had been erected and so had a half-dozen brightly colored pavilions. Their long pennons fluttered in the morning breeze.

The road ended at the gate to the walled city. Inside, hundreds of steep-roofed houses huddled together in violet shadow around a cathedral, its wide square stretching deserted before it. Above the city on the crest of the cliff stood a palace of stone. The rising sun splashed it, its towers glowed apricot against the plum-colored sea.

Wolf and I rested beneath some trees until the city awakened. Then we walked down the hill toward its gate. As we crossed the meadow, I found a piece of rope—a leftover from one of the pavilions. With Wolf's consent, I tied one end of it around his neck; the other end I held in my hand. This, I told him, would make him look more like a dog.

I was not apprehensive about taking Wolf into the city. He was so lame that no one could be afraid of him unless he growled and showed his teeth. I did not think he would do that: his wound was still too painful for him to be belligerent. And then, city people would never know the difference between a wolf and a dog.

Still, we walked toward the gate as quickly as we could so as to give the gatekeeper as little time as possible to examine Wolf.

We need not have been concerned. He was not at all interested in Wolf: his perceptions, I decided shortly, had been dulled and his affability heightened by the contents of a bottle from which he drank deeply as we approached.

"Plenty of time! Plenty of time!" he cried as we drew near. "Not to worry, fair maiden. Plenty of time!"

He smiled widely at me. His little eyes sparkled merrily in his red face. We had nothing to fear from him.

"Plenty of time for what, good gatekeeper?" I asked.

"For the marriage, of course. That's what you come for, isn't it? And what every knight and lady from miles around come for, isn't it? That's why there's not a room to be had anywhere, isn't it? Oh, you've plenty of time—it won't be for two hours yet."

"It must be very important. Whose is it?"

"Why, Prince William's, as if you didn't know as well as I." He laughed. "That's amusing. Highly amusing. Prince William's to the Lady Elaine of Castle Idris. It's no envy I have of him, I must say. Shouldn't care for it at all myself. Shouldn't care for it at all. Great fat young woman she be and not at all comely. I seen her the day she come to the palace. And a picky disposition too, if you ask me. No, no. I—"

"But she was to marry Prince John," I said.

"Yes, well . . . that's a sad tale. A sad tale. Drowned he was at her own castle, and there's many a tale about that. Highly suspicious it was that he went swimming like that all alone and never come back. Oh, there be many a tale about that. Dead and gone and buried he is, and a fine sculpture on his tomb for anyone to see in the cathedral. No, no, it's Prince William that she's marrying today, who was betrothed to the Lady Fulvia. And there's many a tale about that, fair maiden. First Prince John dies mysteriously and then the Lady Fulvia."

The gatekeeper frowned and squinted exaggeratedly at me. Then he raised his bottle to his lips and drank deeply. Setting the bottle aside, he looked in surprise for a moment at the rose at my throat.

Then he continued: *"Mysterious!* Most *mysterious!* Oh, there's many a tale there." He looked suspiciously about and whispered, "Poisoned she was, they say. Poisoned so Prince William could marry the Lady Elaine. Highly suspicious! *Highly* suspicious!"

"Do you know a man whose name is Merlin?"

He glared at me. "Why do you ask, maiden?"

"Well, I don't know. I have heard of him and wondered where he lived."

"He don't live here, no indeed. He lives in Marthen Wood, or so 'tis said." He pointed northward. "In an an-n-n-cient oak tree, or so 'tis said. He's a canny man—a wizard, they say. When he comes riding through my gate with that black cloak of his sailing in the wind and the bats flying about him, I turn my back on him—don't want him looking at me with them evil eyes of his, I don't."

The gatekeeper chuckled and leaned close to whisper in my ear: "But there be one way to tame a wizard. Oh, yes, there be. A beau-u-tiful woman can do it every time. The Lady Bellezza took him off and nobody heard a thing from him. Not until day before yesterday. And then he comes flying back to the palace. The king was looking for him, you see, or so they say. He'll be at the marriage and standing beside the king as big as life, more than likely. You'll see."

"Where is the marriage to be?" I asked. "At the cathedral?"

"At the cathedral at eleven o'clock," the gatekeeper replied, pointing the way. "Follow that street to St. George's Square, where the fountain is, and turn to your left. You'll see the cathedral and its square from there."

I thanked the gatekeeper, and Wolf and I walked on toward St. George's Square. From there we would walk to the cathedral. If Merlin was to be at the marriage, we might see him. I did not know what I would do if we did, but I felt quite certain that if we found him, I would think of something. Perhaps I should simply tell him that my godmother told me to find him. If he was a magician, he would surely know why she had.

As we walked, I thought about Prince John. I could not believe that he was dead. In my mind I could hear him laugh, and I could see his eyes flashing with excitement and joy. How beautiful he had been and how powerful and yet so gentle. Even though I had known him for so short a time, he had given me encouragement and hope. Now news of his death filled me with anguish.

"Why should I feel so badly about it?" I murmured to myself.

Wolf looked up at me inquiringly.

"I knew him for only two days."

Wolf looked at me queerly, almost sheepishly, but

then he looked away to examine St. George's Square.

At first it appeared as deserted as the street behind us had been. Such an important day had been declared a holiday, I decided, and people had slept later than usual and were now breakfasting and dressing for the festivities.

But the square was not entirely deserted: a woman carrying an earthen jar walked toward the fountain and a large cage which stood on a low wooden platform beside it. I was curious about the cage, and since we were in no hurry, Wolf and I walked toward it too. The cage contained an enormous wild boar. I could scarcely believe it, but I felt certain it was the same boar that I had seen so often in the hills above Castle Idris.

The woman arrived at the fountain at the same time we did and, paying no attention to me, began to fill her jar.

"Do you know anything about this animal?" I asked her. "Why is it here?"

"For everyone to see," she replied.

"But— Do you know where it came from?"

"From the forest."

"What will they do with it?"

"Eat it. It's for the marriage feast."

She said no more. Placing the filled jar on her shoulder, she walked away. I watched her until she had disappeared down a narrow street, and Wolf and I were left alone standing before the cage.

The boar gazed at me with the same strange expression that I had seen on its face so many times before. Yes, I was certain that this was the same animal—the one I had saved from Prince John's spear. Though old, he was a magnificent beast. But he would hardly be tender eating. It seemed that he recognized me, for he came to me, sniffed, and looked at me with imploring eyes.

"Poor fellow," I said to him.

I gazed at the boar for some time, trying not to remember how it felt to be caged and about to be eaten and trying not to allow myself to decide what I had decided already. Then I strolled leisurely around the cage, my hands clasped behind me, until I reached its door.

Pretending to admire the ironwork, I ran my hands along the bars, and as I touched the latch, I lifted it and swung the door ajar—far enough so that it would not close again.

Chapter Twenty-six

****

Elaine's Story

Then Wolf and I walked casually away.

The square remained silent and deserted while Wolf and I crossed it. As we entered the street leading to the cathedral, I glanced back at the cage just in time to see the boar leap out of it and dash toward the city gate. Then I heard a cry of alarm and saw a boy run shouting from one of the houses in pursuit.

The cathedral square basked in sunshine, nearly deserted. As Wolf and I entered it and walked toward the cathedral, I thought how perfect a day it was for a marriage—mild and still under the sky's cloudless blue canopy.

Wolf and I chose to wait on the steps of a stone cross which stood before the porch of the great church. Here I could sit down, yet be elevated above the throng and so be able to see without difficulty.

I had no doubt that almost everyone in the city would be gathered in the square by the time the bridal mass began, and crowds of people from the outlying countryside as well. And I was right: long before the bells began to toll the hour, a boisterous mob in holi-day mood had packed the square. They had come to watch the arrival of the lords and ladies and knights who had been invited to attend the ceremony and mass inside the church, and later the appearance of the king and the prince and princess.

Those nobles and landowners who had stayed in the city walked to the church, attended by their squires and gentlemen and gentlewomen, and heralded by their trumpeters as they came. Those who had ridden in that morning left their horses with grooms at the edge of the square and walked to the church porch from there.

The magnificence of their dress awed the multitude. And a hush often fell upon the crowd as they gaped at the silks and velvets and jewels and furs that passed before them and up the steps and through the doors of the cathedral.

Finally the cathedral bells began to toll. At the same time a fanfare of trumpets sounded. One of the women who crowded the cross's steps beside me pointed to the street that descended from the palace and said to her husband, "Here they come!"

"Who?" the man asked.

"The Lady Elaine and her mother."

Every head turned toward my stepmother and step-sister as they rode into view. Only Gloria and Mathilda were mounted. Each rode a snow-white, splendidly caparisoned palfrey. Surrrounding them walked their gentlewomen and gentlemen, wearing the Idris badge. Trumpeters preceded the party, heralding their approach, followed by three footmen, each hold-ing forth a scarlet cushion upon which rested an ob-ject that I could not see.

"What's on them?" the man said, pointing to the footmen.

"Her dowry," the woman said. "The gifts she gives to the king at the marriage."

"Miniver!" cried a woman behind me.

"No it isn't," another woman said. "It's ermine,

and her gown is samite. White samite, by the look of it."

They were talking about Gloria. She did indeed wear a long ermine cloak over her gown. And she wore a gold coronet. My stepmother's cloak was of heavily embroidered gold brocade, her gown of sky-blue velvet.

But though their clothes were appropriate, their attitudes, I thought, were unsuitable. Gloria sat on her horse with an expression of disdain upon her face—as though everything about her coming marriage was unpleasant and inferior. Mathilda simpered and waved to the crowd patronizingly. Both looked smug.

When they reached the steps of the porch, Gloria and Mathilda were helped to dismount. I held my hand in front of my face and watched them from between my fingers. They were not twelve yards away, and I did not want them to see me. But I need not have worried: they were entirely too preoccupied with their own postures to notice anyone in the crowd. Then, preceded by the trumpeters and footmen, the entire party entered the cathedral.

The great doors were closed.

"Where's the king?" an old woman who stood beside me asked. "I want to see the king!"

"He's gone in by the side door," the woman standing with her husband said. "Him and the prince and the princess. They'll come out when it's—"

She did not finish because at that moment her attention was drawn to the church. One of its doors had opened to allow a very short old man with long yellow-gray hair and beard to walk out of the building. He was dressed entirely in black. Now he stood on the porch glaring down at the crowd.

Wolf leaped to the ground, limped through the spectators to the steps of the church, and climbed them to the gray-haired man.

Chapter Twenty-seven

****

Elaine's Story

"Wolf!" I cried, running after him. "Wolf, come here!"

I was forced to push my way rudely through the people, but they did not try to stop me.

It was only after I had climbed to the porch and grasped Wolf's rope that I looked into the man's face and recognized him. He was the little man who had told me the riddle at Castle Idris.

"You are late!" he said to me. "Must you wait until the last minute? Come along!" He walked a few steps toward the partially open door to the cathedral. Then he stopped and looked back at me. "Well? Quickly! Quickly!"

"In there?" I asked. "I couldn't possibly—"

"And you too," he said, looking at Wolf. Then he shut his eyes and shook his head rapidly. "How did you ever—? Never mind, we will put it right somehow. Come along, both of you!"

"I couldn't possibly go in there," I said.

The man ran to me, grasped my hand, and pulled

me toward the door. "There is no time for that. Come!"

Wolf followed him eagerly, and before I knew what had happened, the man had pulled me into the church and some other men had shut the door behind us.

"Come along," the gray-haired man said, striding toward the nave.

I followed him now without question: he, at least, was familiar to me, and I did not want to lose him. Almost at a run, he led me down a narrow aisle which cleaved the throng of resplendent nobles banked on either side of the nave. Their excited chatter roared about us as it echoed and re-echoed from the granite walls. The sun blazed through the huge rose window behind us, and we hurried through shafts of ruby and sapphire light.

We had nearly reached the transept before I could see King Alfred. He sat on a throne toward one side of the choir, swathed in ermine and wearing a heavy jeweled crown. Prince William and Princess Bedrine stood beside him, and so did the archbishop, robed in scarlet. Behind them in a semicircle clustered the dukes and highest born nobles of the kingdom, fawning on the king and quarreling among themselves.

Mathilda and Gloria stood at the steps of the choir behind their footmen, who knelt and extended Gloria's dowry toward the king. He paid no attention to them, being distracted by a richly dressed gentleman who leaned in front of the archbishop to whisper into his ear.

As we walked toward them, a woman darted out of the crowd to the gray-haired man and grasped his hand. She was young and extraordinarily beautiful, with snow-white hair and huge almond-shaped violet eyes.

"Stay with me, Merlin," she cried. "Come, be with me, my dear."

The gray-haired man wrenched his hand from hers and, with an angry glare at the maiden, strode on. Wolf and I followed him.

The girl had called him Merlin. This, then, had to be the magician that Godmother had told me to find.

Now King Alfred saw Merlin and Wolf and me as we drew near. He raised his hand to silence those about him. At the same time my stepmother and Gloria, having followed the king's gaze, stared at me in astonishment. They whispered briefly but frantically together. Then, smiling slightly, Mathilda turned with exaggerated calm back to the king. But Gloria's eyes pursued me in outrage as I followed Merlin up the steps of the choir to the throne.

"What have we here, Merlin?" King Alfred asked.

"This is the Lady Elaine, my liege, daughter of the Duke of Idris," Merlin said.

I curtsied deeply to the king. When I rose and stepped back several paces, I saw that he was examining me with an expression of surprise and disapproval. I did not blame him: I had traveled and slept in my cloak and homespun kirtle, and I had no doubt they looked it.

Finally the king turned his attention to Wolf. As he gazed at the animal, he took a handkerchief from his sleeve and held it to his nose. "What is *that?*" he said to Merlin. "Take it away!"

"Noble sovereign!" Merlin cried. "Look closely, my gracious liege. May not the animal remain?" He looked at my stepmother. "Its presence is of the greatest importance, is it not, lady?"

"I could not say, Merlin," Mathilda said, screwing up her face in her painful smile. "But it would not seem appropriate."

"Precisely!" the archbishop cried. "Your Majesty, I beg you— The sanctity of the sanctuary!"

King Alfred raised his hand for silence. He had reexamined Wolf, as Merlin had urged. Wolf had walked to him and, after gazing up at the king, had sat down at his feet.

Half-puzzled, I thought, half-resigned to the animal, King Alfred gestured impatiently to Merlin to continue.

"Most gracious sovereign," Merlin said loudly so that those surrounding the king as well as those in the front ranks of the assemblage could hear, "Your Grace, Your Highness, Your Eminence, my lords, worthy knights, ladies and gentlemen, this day"—he glanced at the archbishop—"a divine prophecy shall be fulfilled."

The crowd murmured.

King Alfred held up his hand, and Merlin continued: "It has been written that two maidens will come forth this day, each as the Lady Elaine, daughter of the Duke of Idris and the betrothed of His Grace, the crown prince, each for her marriage unto him. Further it is prophesied that each will bring a dowry, and by the worth of that dowry the rightful maiden shall be made known."

The crowd babbled excitedly until at the king's gesture the royal trumpeters played a fanfare.

"We shall have the gifts!" King Alfred commanded.

"If it please your most gracious Majesty," my stepmother cried at once, "my stepdaughter, the Lady Elaine, presents"—she prodded the footman who knelt nearest her with her foot. He ran to the throne, knelt before it, and extended his velvet cushion to the king. On it rested a metal box exactly like the box the hermit had given me to carry to Queen Harmonia—"the treasure of Queen Hecuba," Mathilda shouted triumphantly.

King Alfred seized the chest, placed it in his lap, and attempted to lift its lid. He tugged impatiently at it, but the box would not open. Sheepishly, he replaced the box on its cushion and waved the footman away.

Mathilda announced: "The chest of skilled workmanship, tooled in a superb design of birds and flowers, contains priceless jewels of the highest quality in every size and variety."

The footman bearing the box stepped aside to allow the second footman to kneel before the king. Now King Alfred grasped a flower that lay upon the cushion and examined it.

"A lifelike flower," Mathilda cried, "its petals and leaves carved of the rarest, most costly jade."

The king replaced the flower. The footman rose and stepped aside to allow the third footman to kneel before the throne. On his cushion lay a leather purse very like the purse of the stranger whose wound I had bound.

King Alfred took the purse, opened it, and poured several coins from it into his hand.

"Thirty silver deniers!" Mathilda shouted. "Surely, my liege, this poor child"—she pointed at me—"can offer nothing to compare in value with these, my stepdaughter Elaine's gifts." She smiled intensely. "I beg your most sagacious Majesty to proceed with the marriage."

The king placed the coins and the purse on their cushion and waved the footman away to join the other two standing side by side to the left of the throne. Then King Alfred looked expectantly at Merlin, who stood next to me.

"It is your turn," Merlin whispered to me.

"My turn?" I said.

"To offer your gifts."

"But I have none."

"Of course you have."

"But they are of no value. I couldn't!"

Merlin frowned at me. The bewitchery of his stare compelled obedience.

I slipped the rose from the clasp of my cloak, took the blue glass bottle and the nail out of my purse, and curtsying deeply before King Alfred, offered them to him.

He took my poor gifts, and as I rose, he held up the bottle saying, "What is this?"

Again I curtsied, and from that position, looking at the floor, I said, "The bottle contains the tears of Queen Harmonia, my liege."

Someone behind the king tittered. The titter was joined by someone's chortle. King Alfred threw back

his head and guffawed. Dropping the rose, and the nail
and the bottle, which smashed on the marble floor, he
grasped the sides of his chest and shook with laughter.

Mortified, I rose and ran to Merlin. He ignored
me; his gaze was fastened to the floor at the king's feet.
He left me, knelt before the king, and seemed to pick
up fragments of the glass bottle.

Then, offering them to King Alfred in his open
palm, he said, "Do these amuse you so greatly, my
liege?"

Several lords who stood behind the king gasped, and
the king stopped laughing to gaze wide-eyed into Merlin's palm. There lay three tear-shaped diamonds.
They were as large as fingernails, perfectly matched,
and blazed with such fire that I wondered if they might
burn the flesh. The king extended his hand, and
Merlin dropped them into it.

"Where did you get these, child?" the king asked
me.

"I— The bottle was given to me by Queen Harmonia, Your Majesty," I said. "One day I came upon
a hermit who asked me to deliver Queen Hecuba's
treasure to her because he could not do it himself. It
was in a little chest exactly like the one on the cushion
there." I gestured to Gloria's box. "When I gave it to
Queen Hecuba, she told me her name was really
Queen Harmonia, and she gave me the bottle in gratitude and as part of my dowry. She said it contained
some of her tears."

Now Merlin stood, took Gloria's box from the footman, and holding it in his hands, asked my stepmother,
"How came you by this chest, lady?"

"It has been in our family for generations, Merlin,"
she replied, smiling.

Merlin grasped the lid of the chest, raised it, and
gazed into the open box. Then he turned it upside
down. Pebbles bounced and rattled onto the floor.

"Pebbles! Common stones!" he cried, glaring at
Mathilda. "The sea casts them upon our shores by the

millions. Is this the treasure you give His Majesty, lady?"

Without waiting for her answer, he picked up the jade flower. "And how came you by this stone flower, lady?" he asked.

"It was given to us!" Gloria cried. "It was given to us by a strange yellow-skinned man."

"Be quiet!" Mathilda whispered.

But Gloria paid no attention to her mother. "At first he offered us a common rose," she continued, "and other common flowers, but we could accept only a flower befitting our station; so he gave us that one of jade, which was the finest he had."

Now Merlin picked up my rose and the nail from the floor. "How came you by this rose, maiden?" he said to me.

"It was given to me by a yellowish-skinned, foreign-looking man," I said. "He offered it to me, and when I said I could not pay him for it, he told me it was a gift for my dowry. I love the wild roses; they are my favorite flower."

"And how long have you had the blossom?" Merlin asked.

"Nearly a week, I think."

"How have you kept it?"

"I have worn it—in the clasp of my cloak. It has perfumed my way."

Merlin gave the rose to King Alfred. "See how fresh it is, my liege. And smell its perfume. Could it have been plucked from its bush before this morning? Why, the dew has scarcely dried upon its petals. But from whence came this rose in the midst of winter, when its bush lies brown and leafless beneath the snow?"

The king looked up at Merlin, mystified.

"It is a magic flower, my liege. It will remain forever fresh. It will never die."

Merlin turned to my stepmother then and said to her, "And how came you by these silver coins, lady?"

"It is our money," Mathilda said. "Good Merlin, why do you ask when it is none if your concern?"

Then Merlin turned to me and said, "And how came you by this nail, maiden?"

"It was given to me by a man whom I found wounded by the roadside," I said. "He had been cut about the forehead and was bleeding from a wound in his side. He offered me his purse if I would bind his wound and help him to an inn. The purse was very like that one"—I gestured to the purse that held the silver coins—"but I said I could not accept it. Then I bound his wound and helped him down the road until twelve of his friends appeared to care for him. He gave me the nail and said to take it in remembrance of him and that it was to be a part of my dowry."

"This man was cut about the forehead and was wounded in the side, you say?" Merlin asked.

"Yes."

"Was he wounded on the hands or feet?"

"I do not— I do not know. He wore boots and gloves."

Merlin examined the nail for a moment. Then he handed it to the king.

"See, my liege—the end of the nail."

King Alfred held the nail in his right hand and bent toward it. Almost at once he cupped the palm of his left hand under the nail's point. Suddenly there appeared in his palm a spot of red. The spot grew larger. With a glance, the king summoned the archbishop's attention.

"What drips from the nail, Your Majesty?" the archbishop asked.

King Alfred handed the nail to the archbishop. He examined it in awe, strode to the altar, and placed the nail upon it.

Turning to the king, he shouted, "It bleeds, my liege!" He ran back to the throne, pointed to the altar, and cried breathlessly, "See the altar! See the cloth upon it. It is red with blood. The blood of our Lord! It is a nail from the cross. It is a miracle!"

He rushed back to the altar and threw himself upon

his knees before it. Then I realized that the sun outside the cathedral was darkening. In the dusk the multitude sank to its knees. I knelt too. Then all about us voices of a celestial choir swelled in praise of the Lord.

Chapter Twenty-eight

✠✠✠✠✠✠✠✠✠✠✠✠✠✠✠✠✠✠✠✠

Elaine's Story

When the voices were silent and the sun shone through the windows again, Merlin rose. Turning to King Alfred, he said, "Know you now, my liege, the true betrothed? Has not our Lord been with us here today, as this child"—he gestured to me—"was with Him by the roadside to bind His wound? And did He not also appear to that lady"—he pointed to my stepmother—"and her daughter, Gloria, and did He not reward them with thirty pieces of silver for leaving Him to die, just as Judas was paid the like amount to betray Him?

"And in choosing the humble rose, was not the Lady Elaine justly rewarded with a bloom of everlasting life, while the Lady Gloria's pride begot a dead flower of stone? A wise man of the East once said, 'What the superior man seeks is in himself. What the mean man seeks is in others.' Does he not speak to us with these two flowers?

"And were not the queen's diamond tears a prize worthy of the Lady Elaine's honor, while that lady"—

he pointed at Gloria—"believing she had, in her deceit and envy, stolen the queen's jewels, received only seaside pebbles in their stead?

"Does not a lesson for all of us lie in this? The maiden of kindness, honor, and humility is the true Lady Elaine of Castle Idris." He pointed at me. "There stands the daughter of the Duke of Idris, and our future queen!"

I cried then, not only because I had been vindicated, but because my father and Prince John were not there with me. But my tears had barely blurred my sight when my stepmother distracted me: she ran, as best she could with her twisted leg, toward the nave of the church.

"Seize her!" the king commanded.

Two guards ran after Mathilda and grasped her arms. But suddenly their hands were empty: my stepmother had vanished. The king, Merlin, everyone, saw it, and each person in that great church held his breath as the air hung still with incredulity.

Then a crash and a horrible shrill scream rent the air. A hole gaped in the center of the rose window at the rear of the cathedral. A body materialized, fell through the air, and landed with a thud among shattering fragments of glass on the stone floor.

Women shrieked and men shouted. King Alfred jumped up and strode, followed by Merlin, toward the commotion, a path through the crowd opening before him.

I watched them for a moment, but then my eyes were drawn back to the throne. Prince John stood naked beside it, a rope encircling his neck and falling against his body. I ran to him and threw my cloak about him. He laughed, wrapped his arm around me, and held me tightly against him. In this way we waited for his father and Merlin to return.

Gloria waited, too, I noticed. She stood still, staring toward the rear of the cathedral and holding a long-haired snow-white cat in her arms. The cat seemed terrified and struggled to escape.

Finally she was no longer able to hold it, and as King Alfred and Merlin approached the choir, the cat leaped from her and darted away.

The king walked directly to Gloria and spoke to her. Merlin came to John and me.

"Well, that is a relief, isn't it?" he said to John. Then to me he said, "It was your stepmother. She is dead."

I looked at Gloria and the king then. King Alfred saw John for the first time. He ran to his son and embraced him. I went to Gloria. I was sure that King Alfred had told her about her mother: she seemed so pathetically crestfallen and bewildered as she stood all alone. I felt unbearably sorry for her.

"Gloria," I said, taking both her hands in mine, "I am so sorry. Stay with us. Let us help you."

Gloria looked disdainfully at me, disengaged her hands, turned, and walked down the nave toward the body of her mother.

I returned to John, the king, and Merlin.

"We shall perform the marriage as originally planned," King Alfred was saying to Merlin and John. "We must begin at once! We will have the tournament and the marriage feast! These good people"—he gestured to the congregation—"have gathered for a marriage and a bridal mass. They must not be disappointed or kept waiting any longer."

Then King Alfred turned to me. "In the absence of your father, Elaine," he said, "I appoint the archbishop your guardian. He shall perform the marriage."

The king strode to the altar, where the archbishop knelt in prayer still, to inform him of this. I gazed questioningly up at John.

"Do you object to the marriage?" he asked, looking intently into my eyes. "We have been betrothed since children. Your father and mine were old friends."

"Oh, no!" I cried. "I should love to marry you, John. It would make me very happy. But"—I glanced down at the rough sheepskin vest I had made—"how can I be married in this? And you— you have only my cloak, which is barely large enough to cover you."

I looked about them, certain that every eye was upon us, but in the confusion caused by Mathilda's death, no one seemed to be paying any attention to John and me. No one, that is, except a tiny, bent old woman with white hair and clawlike hands.

Our eyes met, and she smiled at me—my godmother! Suddenly I felt lighter. I looked down at my vest, but it was gone. Tiny pearls lay scattered across my breast and shoulders, sewn there with threads of gold upon a gown of creamy silk.

John now wore chain mail of burnished steel beneath a scarlet surcoat; jewels flashed from a scabbard at his hip.

We were married then, and after the bridal mass, John and I led the procession down the nave of the church. Mathilda's body had been carried away, but we passed the spot where it had lain and then walked out onto the porch to face the multitude in the square. A thunder of cheers buffeted us as we emerged. And as the cathedral bells pealed and the cries of jubilation surged about us, I saw a man pushing his way through the crowd toward the porch steps. He ran up to me and I threw my arms about him.

"Father!" I cried through my tears. "Father! Oh, Father!"

He clasped me tightly to him, and then, holding me away to examine me, he said, "Elaine, dearest daughter. My God, I thought this would never happen."

We could not talk more then, but I held his hand tightly until we had acknowledged the homage of the throng and were walking in procession behind the king, John on my right and Father on my left, toward the palace.

Then, looking at the torn, soiled cloak he wore, I said, "Where have you been? Why didn't you come back?"

"Very near you," Father said, smiling at me. "I am sorry for my poor clothes. These rags were all I could find. But earlier this morning you were not dressed so magnificently, either."

"How do you know that?"

"Because I saw you."

"And you didn't speak? Where were you?"

"In a cage beside the fountain. And if you had not opened it for me, I should not be with you now."

Chapter Twenty-nine

✳✳✳✳✳✳✳✳✳✳✳✳✳✳✳✳✳✳✳✳✳

Elaine's Story

I was so perplexed by the events of the past two hours that when we arrived at the palace, I begged Father and Merlin to come at once to our chamber with John and me, and explain them.

"You were the boar in the cage?" I asked Father when we were all seated comfortably together.

"Yes, Elaine," he said. "Mathilda changed me into a boar soon after we arrived at Castle Idris ten years ago. I stayed near you in the hills, wanting to help. But what could I do? Then, because of this young man's tales, I suppose"—he smiled at John—"a hunting party captured me, and I would have been slaughtered this morning for the marriage banquet if you had not let me out of the cage."

"Slaughtered, but not eaten," Merlin said, his eyes glinting.

"How could she have changed Father into a boar?" I asked. "And why not eaten?"

"Because once transformed into another being by Mathilda," Merlin said, "only Mathilda or death could return that person to his original form—his own death or hers. So you see, if your father, as the boar, had been killed, he would in death at once have reverted in form to his own body.

"Mathilda was a sorceress of considerable power," Merlin continued, "as was her mother before her until she was turned to gold by the Queen of the Caves. It was with the gold of her mother's body that Mathilda attracted and married the Duke of Straggore, Gloria's father.

"He disappeared during the siege of Castle Deleans. No one knew where he had gone until his body was found naked at the gates after the castle fell. Probably Mathilda had turned him into a war horse before she fled with a knight whose name was Tor Malafie."

"She fled to Wales," Father said to me, "where your mother and I met her. I believe she poisoned your mother, but Mathilda was so kind and consoling after her death that I was blinded to her nature. I did not realize how cruel she was until she had changed me into an animal. I believe she gave me enchanted wine to drink."

"With a drop of her own blood in it," Merlin said. "That was the way she cast her spell. Her powers were threefold: First, she could, as we have said, transform any person or animal into whatever being she wished, provided, of course, he drank a drop of her blood in wine, or milk, or water, or whatever. She could, I believe, transform herself too. But that would have been extremely dangerous, and I do not believe she would consider doing so without great provocation. Second, she knew the secret of transferring herself invisibly from one place to another at will—no matter how great the distance. And third, she possessed the ability to watch and listen to events taking place anywhere by looking into the reflection of still water. And though disguise is not a supernatural power, she was a master of it.

"But like all sorceresses, her powers had their limits. And since all life must balance out, to compensate for these powers, she was denied certain capacities and abilities of more normal persons: She was denied the ability to love or feel kindness or compassion. And she was denied the joy of giving without extracting in kind more than the gift was worth. She was also denied the ability to feel sorrow and the solace of tears. And physically, of course, she was ugly and lame."

"But why was she so intent on Gloria's marriage to John or Prince William?" I asked.

"She planned to be the power behind the throne," John said. "Can you imagine what it would have been like if she had killed William or turned him into some poor creature? Gloria, as queen, would then have obeyed her mother."

"She had a rapacious appetite for luxury," Merlin said. "She would have bled the people of their wealth for her own pleasures."

"Did you know this when you came to Castle Idris?" I asked Merlin.

"I knew many things about Mathilda," Merlin said. "And when John returned to Tintagal and told me about the two Elaines, I surmised even more."

"I thought you were safe," John said, "or I would never have left you."

"So you came to Castle Idris to see for yourself?" I asked Merlin.

Merlin smiled at me. "Yes, I wished to see for myself." He chuckled. "The answers to my riddle told me much, but I wished to be certain. That is why I appeared to both you and Gloria as your father."

"It was *you?*" I asked.

"Yes. And then I knew, of course. I returned to Tintagal, and searching for it, discovered the prophecy amongst my books and scrolls. Then I bade John return to Castle Idris and carry you to safety. Unfortunately Mathilda knew that the boar was still alive and therefore that the man Gloria thought was the Duke of Idris was not him, but an impersonation. She suspected me and must have watched while I spoke to

John and listened to our conversation in reflected water.

"So, Mathilda had to rid herself of my interference and John's too. She was a shrewd and dangerous woman. I did not underestimate her for a moment, but I did not think her cunning enough to have created the Lady Bellezza (out of what, I cannot imagine; a cat, perhaps). That lady was as sly as she was beautiful, a woman who quite cast a spell upon me, which only at the last moment was I able to shatter."

"Then, to be rid of me," John said, "Mathilda changed me into a wolf. She must have reasoned that if I was killed by a shepherd or hunter, my body would be found far from Castle Idris and that then she could not possibly be involved."

"And she placed John's clothes on the shore," Merlin said, "to imply that he had drowned. It was only by accident that a fisherman's body resembling John's was cast up on the beach, to be returned to Tintagal for burial.

"I was not unduly worried when I returned to the city: nothing could prevent the prophecy from being fulfilled. I informed His Majesty about it, and persuaded him to say nothing to Mathilda and to proceed with the marriage as planned. And the rest you know."

"What happened at the cathedral?" I asked. "I do not understand how the window was broken."

"After she and Gloria had been exposed," Merlin said, "Mathilda, fearing the king's wrath, went into transference. But though invisible, she was caught in an enclosed space; her only escape lay in breaking through a window. She slashed her throat on broken glass and fell dead on the floor. Death, you see, produced her materialization.

"And with her death, those whom she had transformed returned to their natural state too. Consequently John and your father became men again."

"And the men who gave me my dowry?" I asked. "Who were they? Did you create them, Merlin?"

"No! No, my child. I did not create them." Merlin
fell into deep thought for a moment. Then he said,
"There are powers abroad of which we have no
knowledge. They work within a fabric of mysterious
design. From its form we know it is of goodness made
and not of evil. Those men were threads of that design. I cannot tell you more."

Merlin and Father left John and me then, and
when we were alone, I asked, "Who is he, John?"

"Merlin?" John said. "A wise man. Some say the
son of the devil and a nun. He is a magician and seer
of terrible powers. But . . ."

"Yes?"

"He is said to have one fatal flaw."

"What is that?"

"Since he was born of a mortal, he is drawn to
beautiful women. He told me once that he will die because of one."

"Do you believe him?"

"Yes." John looked at me thoughtfully for a moment. Then he asked, "Did you know that I was
Wolf?"

"No, I did not know. I thought about it, but I could
not believe it was possible. But then, yes, I did believe it—because I wanted to. What was it like? How
did she do it?"

"It was like *being* a wolf in everything physical—
hearing, moving, howling, smelling—but at the same
time, thinking like a man. It was rather terrifying."
He grinned at me. "She gave me a glass of wine to
drink, and all of a sudden I wasn't a man any longer.

"But it had its compensations: I was able to follow
you and Sir Tor by smell. You have no idea how well
a wolf can smell, especially when the trail is fresh.
Mathilda changed me into a wolf the day I came back
to Castle Idris, and that was the day Sir Tor took
you away."

"That was why he did it so quickly," I said. "They
had to get me away before you came to me. They
must have planned it together, however hastily. I was

to die on Mortmoor. But then she must have seen
that we were alive by gazing into the still waters of
the fishpond at Castle Idris. I saw her there once and
remember wondering about it. What, by the way,
frightened the shepherd so?"

"You don't know?"

"No, what?"

"He thought you were a werewolf."

"He did?" I began to laugh.

"He would have killed me if you hadn't stepped
between us. That was not amusing."

"And Sir Tor would have killed me and the dragon
would have, too, if you hadn't killed them first. Dame
Winet was Mathilda in disguise, wasn't she?"

"Yes," John said. "I tried to warn you—to make
you leave—but you wouldn't listen. So I left the barn
and kept watch by the steps."

"How did you know Dame Winet was Mathilda?
I did not know it at the time."

"By her smell."

"Do you know I never saw her walk? She always
stood still or sat. I would have known she was
Mathilda if I had seen her limp."

"Yes, and she was the woman in the village who
cried 'Wolf.' "

"She must have changed herself into the wolf that
killed a little boy that morning. That was why everyone was out looking for a wolf, which they thought
was you."

"I wonder," John said, "that she did not kill you
herself."

"She tried," I replied. "She knew where I was. She
drew the picture, and wrote the poem, and left them
in the giant's hut. No one else could have gone there
and escaped, but she could have: she appeared in an
instant, laid the paper on the table, and disappeared
as quickly as she had come."

"I mean with her bare hands."

"She probably would have if she could have found

us after that. But we hid in the daytime and traveled only at night, when she could not see us.

"She was horrible!" I continued. "She *deceived* everyone. She purposely played the distrait fool in order to take advantage of others."

"She is dead," John said. "We must not allow her to blight our lives." He walked to a door and opened it. It led to a balcony. He stepped out onto it, extended his hand to me, and said, "Come."

I went to him. He wrapped his arms around me and kissed me. Then, holding me close, he gazed out across the city.

"All this is your kingdom, Princess Elaine," he said. "Those mountains, those fields and woods, the shore, the city, this palace, this person, this heart."

The End of Elaine's Story

Afterword

✠✠✠✠✠✠✠✠✠✠✠✠✠✠✠✠✠✠✠✠✠

This part of Elaine's story, then, is finished. Perhaps, typical of such tales, its last few words should be "and they lived happily ever after." For us that is true if we make believe.

Actually, according to Sir Thomas Malory and other chroniclers of Arthurian legends, John lived for only a few years longer. He was killed during the siege of the castle of Terrabil when still a young man. Thereby hangs a tale of skulduggery, during which Merlin was responsible for Elaine's, or to use her more familiar name, Igraine's, marriage to Uther Pendragon. She then bore a child, Arthur, destined to become perhaps the greatest king of legend and song.

As his reward for arranging the marriage, Merlin demanded of Uther that Igraine's child be given to him to be brought up as he saw fit. Uther agreed and this was done. Before coming upon Igraine's and Gloria's stories, I had always wondered how Igraine felt about having her child taken from her and given to Merlin. In spite of her husband's authority, did she not object violently to this? But I think now, because of the events in our story, that she owed Merlin a debt and that repaying it with her child mitigated her loss.

All this is idle speculation. But it is no speculation to say that Lord Toddingdale's account of Mathilda's death inside the cathedral is a fabrication. In those days marriages were not performed inside a church: they were performed either at home or outside the church in front of its doors. Therefore Mathilda would not have killed herself by attempting to escape through a window of the cathedral: she would never have entered the building in the first place. It is for this reason that I believe the following version of her death, found among Lord Toddingdale's papers, is a translation of the original manuscript and therefore the authentic account of it.

Since Igraine's manuscript is lost, let me try to set the scene for all this: Gloria and Prince William march in procession from the palace, together with King Alfred and his court, and now they all stand on the porch of the cathedral, joined by the archbishop. Merlin appears at the last minute, shrugs off Bellezza, who tries to interfere, Wolf and Elaine go to him, just as they did in our story, and the gifts are presented to the king, there on the steps. The sun darkens and the celestial choir sings, and Elaine is proclaimed the true daughter of the Duke of Idris.

Lord Toddingdale's translated fragment begins with Merlin's final speech, just as it appears in our story, and then Elaine continues her narrative in the first person:

"Does not a lesson for all of us lie in this? The maiden of kindness, honor, and humility is the true Lady Elaine of Castle Idris. There stands the daughter of the Duke of Idris, and our future queen!"

I cried then, not only because I had been

vindicated, but because my father and Prince
John were not there with me, but at the same
time I was terribly uneasy about Sir Hugh, who
had thrown the spear that wounded. Wolf so
grievously.

He had, as I have said, come to the city for
the marriage and the tournament, and now
stood near the steps of the porch with his squire
beside him. The squire clutched Sir Hugh's
spear. He and Sir Hugh had whispered more
and more excitedly to each other as Gloria's
and my gifts had been presented to the king.
Because of his attitude, I was certain now that
Sir Hugh recognized Wolf, and was eager to
kill him.

But Wolf would be safe as long as he remained sitting at the feet of the king and in the
midst of such a large group of people. Somehow, I thought, I must keep him surrounded
by people until we had got out of Sir Hugh's
sight. I could not plan, however, how I was going to manage this because I did not know
what would happen next.

It was Merlin who spoke to Mathilda then:
"Release our young lord, His Grace, from thy
spell, lady. It is worth nothing to you now."

"I have no idea of what you speak, Merlin,"
Mathilda said with a smile of triumph. "Spell?
I am but a poor old woman, ill used. I know
nothing of spells." Then grasping Gloria's hand,
she said to her daughter loudly enough for all
to hear, "Come, my dear, let us leave His Majesty and those about him to their fate. He will,
I think, be glad to see us go."

They descended the steps then, and as they
reached the pavement, Wolf raised his head and
howled. The sound was piercing and drew
everyone's attention to him. Then, growling
loudly, Wolf leaped after Mathilda. He ran as

fast as he could down the steps toward her, and
with a vicious snarl prepared to pounce.

Mathilda saw him, and as Wolf sprang, she
threw herself between him and Sir Hugh, crying, "No! No, not the doggie!"

But she was too late to forestall Sir Hugh:
already his spear flew through the air. It struck
Mathilda, impaling her heart.

She fell to the ground. Beside her, naked,
stood Prince John, a rope falling against his
body from a loop encircling his neck. I ran to
him and threw my cloak about him. He laughed,
wrapped his arm around me, and held me close
to him.

That is the end of Lord Toddingdale's other version of Mathilda's death. I suppose that then Elaine
tries to comfort Gloria, who has found her cat, and
as we have read, Gloria shuns Elaine, and Elaine and
Prince John are married.

One other sentence, written in Lord Toddingdale's
own hand on a separate sheet of paper, is attached
to this fragment. I do not understand it, but I quote
it here, hoping that it may have meaning to some of
my readers:

It was not about a story child, but of John,
and my choice was right excepting one: I should
have said, "A sword."

Bestsellers from BALLANTINE